ENSLAVED BY A MAFIA BOSS
1

Brickhouse

ISBN: 978-1-955235-07-5

DEDICATION

To my husband, Derrick. Thank you so much for your sacrifice. You have my back through whatever and I will always adore you for that. Thank you for not complaining the long nights I'm on this computer chasing a dream that's larger than I ever imagined. You're irreplaceable.

Love You Forever And Then After That!

Your Apple Spice.

Enslaved By A Mafia Boss: Book One.
Copyright 2021 Phoenix Publishing House,
Brickhouse. All rights reserved.
Published in the United States of America.

This novel is a work of fiction. Any references to
real people, events, establishments, or locales are
intended only to give the fiction a sense of reality
or authenticity. Other names, characters, and
incidents occurring in the work are either
product of the author's imagination or are used
fictitiously, as are those fictionalized events and
incidents that involve real persons. Any
character that happens to share the name of a
person who is any acquaintance of the author,
past or present, is purely coincidental and is in
no way intended to be an actual account
involving that person. The publisher does not
have any control and does not assume any
responsibility for author or third-party websites.

Published by Phoenix Publishing House, LLC.
ISBN-13: 978-1-955235-04-4

Published by:
PHOENIX PUBLISHING HOUSE
P.O. Box 154855
Lufkin, TX 75904

ABOUT THE AUTHOR

Life is already the hardest it can be, so Brickhouse loves to escape into the fictional worlds she creates. With new books always in the making, she invites her readers to join her in her escape. Her passion for writing dates back to her childhood when she would copy her favorite books word for word and staple the pages together.

Although her greatest inspiration stems from her ability to create worlds where she can be in total control, she will always fondly remember her 7th-grade teacher's inspirational words: *'you have a way with words, and one day it will make you famous'.*

Brickhouse is excited to embark on this journey of writing with readers around the world.
She currently lives in Lufkin, Texas, with her family. She is the owner of Phoenix Publishing House and Phoenix Notary Services.

Feel free to connect with her via:
Instagram: @author_brickhouse
Facebook: Author Brickhouse

SYNOPSIS

Family ties often can be entirely too strong, significantly when you're raised in the mafia. Averly Grace, the "whatever you say, daddy," princess of the Saccone empire, ran off with her fiancé, Grecia years ago, to live the life she wanted. This was her only attempt to find real love, and she was determined not to let her father tell her how to live her life until she found out that her father's wishes were for her to marry someone else to save the family. She knows nothing about this man or what type of trouble her father has gotten himself into, but if she walks away, she'll be disowned, and like most daddy's girls, she's not prepared to lose her father.

Lexington Charles, the Mamba Clan prince, is the son of a narcissist who will do anything, including selling his son's hand to marry into Averly Grace's family for status that he was duped out of long ago. Lexington has been living his own life, still overseeing the business, but if he doesn't take Averly Grace's hand, their empire could stagnate.

Lexington's father has looked down on him for so long for dating Chasity, a woman ignorant of the "life". Still, Lexington will put his pride to the side for the Italian/African-American Averly Grace, who will hopefully bring absolute honor and esteem to his family's name. This union could solidify his father in the unground world and grant access to some coveted connections.

The unsavory lifestyles aren't the only thing these two families have in common. They've been harboring a secret that only the enemy of their families knows, which could forge an alliance or cause a war. Averly Grace and Lexington have no choice but to get married, but can they remain loyal to one another in the face of adversity when it comes to choosing between their family or the truth? The only way out for all parties seems to be death or dishonor, which can be the same in the Enslaved by a Mafia Boss Series.

CHAPTER ONE

AVERLY GRACE

"Averly Grace, you knew this day was coming. Now get prepared."

My father ended the call the way he did when he didn't want to hear any rebuttals from me.

My stomach was tangled in knots and my heart was slowly sinking like quicksand.

I was starting to feel light-headed as I paced back and forth, clutching my stomach.

How am I supposed to tell Grecia what I have to do?

I went into the laundry room and pulled my cleaning supplies from the shelf.

I grew more irritated as I stormed through the house, looking for something to take my frustrations out on.

I hated that our cleaning service had beat me to the job.

I dropped the bucket by the bedroom door and went into our closet. I sat on the red velvet chaise and took a deep breath.

The only thing I could do was rearrange my closet. Nothing was out of order, just the way Grecia liked it.

He was plagued by obsessive-compulsive disorder. Certain things sent him into a rant if they were not a particular way.

As I arranged my clothes, by designer, then color, I scolded myself internally for not being able to tell my father no. I wish I were strong enough to fight back or stand up to him, but I couldn't. It would ruin everything, not only for me but for my family.

Besides, if I were going to tell my father no, I would've done so already. I weighed every possible outcome, and none of them work out in my favor.

I've never felt so defeated in my life.
It took me about an hour to organize our closet. I decided to head downstairs.

I rubbed my hands across the black marble counters. Everything in our home was customized. The marble was flown in from Italy. The designer we selected was elated that he didn't have a budget.

Grecia knew I came from money. He wanted to make sure I maintained my lifestyle and prove to my father that he could take care of me.

I pulled an already open bottle of red wine from the refrigerator and filled my goblet. I grabbed the bottle and tucked it under my arm as I made my way to the couch.

I heard the lock click three times. I knew it was Grecia. He had to click the lock threefold before entering our home.

I missed him when he had to travel, but I also indulged in my time alone.

Three was his number of completion. He would repeat this pattern in various situations. When he kissed me, it was three soft pecks before snaking his tongue down my throat. When opening the refrigerator, he would pull it open and shut it three times.

"Heeey baby," he kissed me his systematic three times before showing me how much he missed me.

The smell of the roses was potent. I hated roses, but after constantly reminding Grecia of this, I decided just to let it go.

"These must be fresh," I took a deep inhale before pulling them from his arms. "What are these for?"

Our relationship is complicated. Grecia is not mean, but he's not your typical man that brings roses home after a long day of selling drugs.

He does have a mean streak that frightens me from time to time.

I tried to determine if he was genuine or done something stupid he was trying to butter me up to receive.

"I missed you the past few days I've been out of town. Isn't that enough?"

"I guess."

"You know I had to go and check them cats out before I let them jump down with my team.

He rambled on about his trip and how he believes the new addition would add tons of revenue from their area. He was as excited about the expansion.

Most of the city was run by my father and the other mob families, but Grecia still managed to make the small sector they didn't dominate work to his advantage. It was smart to expand outside the city if he could handle it.

He was able to strike a deal with the Rufino family. The boss' son Tonio proposed to me, but I declined his offer. His family was rumored to be behind killing my mother because my father refused to let them have a seat at the table.

I watched his lips move, but all I could think about was how our time together had been cut short. I didn't want to spend what moments we have left arguing about something inevitable.

For now, I pushed it to the back of my mind.

Wrapping my arms around his neck, I pulled him close into my embrace.

"Thank you for coming back home to me," my tongue dipped between the seams of his lips. "I love you with everything in me."

"You know I will always come back to you, my Saving Grace," he scooped me up so that my legs were wrapped around his waist.

Desire took over, turning my mind to mush. Grecia knew his way around this body. For that, I was grateful.

When we first started dating, he substituted my first name of Averly with Saving. He said I gave him something to live for. He said I made him want to work towards getting out of the game and retire. He has yet to follow through on those utterances he whispers as we make love.

I thought he was taking me upstairs. Instead, he laid me on the steps.

"You are gorgeous," his gaze devoured me just as passionately as his lips on my thigh.

I could feel myself melting, evaporating into the carpet in a puddle of yearning and liquid lust.

Grecia showed me for a little over an hour how much he missed me the past few days.

"If you would've called me, I could've had dinner ready for you, baby."

That's because I want to cook for you for a change.

"You must've really missed me," I laughed.

"Think I didn't when I did!" He jerked his head back.

"No, baby, you know I love cooking for you. Let me pull myself out this sex juice."

"You gotta cook naked, though," he bit down on his bottom lip.

"Oh, it's about to be one of those nights, huh?"

"Most definitely," the three kisses were slower this time. More sensual than the ones before.

The real reason I didn't want him to cook was that I was too nervous to eat. When I cooked, I rarely ate my cooking. Grecia knew this about me already. A scream sliced through the fog in my brain.

I need to tell him! But why ruin your last moments arguing, Averly? Y'all will be doing that tomorrow morning.

While pulling the chicken breast out of the refrigerator, I could hear Al Green's *Let's Stay Together* blaring from the speakers.

I, I'm so in love with you
Whatever you want to do is alright with me
'Cause you make me feel so brand new
And I want to spend my life with you

Let me say that since, baby, since we've been together
Ooh, loving you forever is what I need
Let me be the one you come running to
I'll never be untrue

Grecia slid behind me as I rinsed the meat off with water and vinegar, "I love seeing you in the kitchen after I sexed you down. Make me feel like Jodie from *Baby Boy*. Did I put it down like that, bae?"

"You know you did, now move so I can get done with dinner," my shove was non-existent against his barreled chest.

He started grinding his hips behind me while his hands were wrapped tightly around my waist.

"What's gotten into you?"

"I can't just be missing you?"

"I guess."

He was overly affectionate and nice, which is out of character for him. I wasn't sure if I should be happy or scared.

If this nigga cheated on me, I swear to God I'm going to rip his balls off and put them in my Ninja blender.

"Lord, if this man is plotting to kill me, just say that," I murmured under my breath.

"What, baby?"

"Nothing, love."

Grecia is a big-time drug dealer. He was never taught how to love a woman. What he knows is what I've managed to teach him over the three years of us being together.

He can be hard sometimes because that's the only way he knows to be. We both had money when we got together.

I'm the daughter of Neri Saccone, the Boss of Bosses. Back in the day, my grandfather was a part of the Dixie Mafia. They had one rule, "Thou shalt not snitch to the cops."

Once he settled in Texas, he put down roots in Houston. Slowly, he recruited other Italian families. A total of four made up the community: the Saccone's, Berlusconi's, Brambilla's, and Ferrari's. One member from each of those families made up *The Council*. My father served as a proxy in my grandfather's stead.

It was one of the reasons he was rushing me to marry. He needed someone to take his spot running the day-to-day so that he could sit on *The Council*. They had the real power, and my father wanted in on it.

My father was adamant about me not dating anyone outside of the connection. I eventually got tired of him trying to control me and decided to go rogue. He didn't think Grecia and I would last this long. Nobody did, not even me.

I've never allowed myself to fall in love with Grecia, but I do love him if that makes sense. I always knew this day would come.

The day I would be called upon to abandon what I wanted and do what my father required.

What makes the drug game and the mafia game different is the family bond. Family is everything in the mafia. You never go against family no matter what.

Because of that and the fact that my gut tells me that he's hiding something, I've kept Grecia at somewhat of a distance.

I've also never been fond of his temper. Sometimes he puts his hands on me. The look in his eyes is only what I can describe as demonic.

It's my mother's fault I'm such a pushover. Her name was Elenor. She was always so sweet and kind. It didn't matter how much of a monster the person was. She continuously operated in a love I've never witnessed before or after her.

She was like the Princess Diana of the mafia families. She held everything together in times of chaos with her kind words, exceptional problem-solving, and easy disposition. The love she had for me and my father was unshakeable. At least that's what Juanita told me. To this day, I have no idea where she is buried with no valid explanation from my father.

When she was murdered, it changed my father forever. I witnessed the life drain from his body when he received the news. It was a car accident, but we found out her car was tampered with. Who would be so bold as to lay a finger on the wife of Neri Saccone?

It's the reason I hold on to my good nature. I pray that it will one day spark him back to life. When I look into his eyes, I wish he could see a part of my mother still here. I hoped that he would come back to life for me.

I refuse to give up on him because I know my mother wouldn't. I have to believe that the monster I've survived is only a shell around the papa I once adored.

My father treats me like property because he bankrolls everything in my life. Grecia takes excellent care of me, but my father refuses to be outdone.

I also would rather be indebted to my dad than I would a man.

He has funded more failed business attempts than I can count. First, it was a clothing boutique, and then it was hair.

I quickly found out that my attitude was not built appropriately to deal with my melinated sisters and their hair.

It just wasn't worth the headache. I wanted something to show for my life, but I was still trying to find my niche.

For now, the only thing I seemed to excel at was conducting meetings, handling my father's business, and doing whatever he tells me to do. I've been learning the ins and outs since I was fourteen years old.

I've never had time for hobbies, so I'm not sure what I liked. Everything in my life was purposed and planned for me.

Dating Grecia started as a form of rebellion. I felt like I had no control over my life. In desperation, I grabbed hold of Grecia, and it stuck longer than I thought it would. Apparently, longer than my father thought it would either.

My father kept me in private school and sent me to a small college to further my education.

That's how I met Grecia. I pulled up to the pump next to him. I noticed how rough around the edges he was.

His cinnamon skin was smooth and his face hard like stone. His countenance looked as if the scowl was engraved into his features.

"What you staring at?"

I remember it like yesterday, him barking this question at me.

I jumped and quickly lowered my head as I pumped my gas.

"I'm just messing with you. I'm Grecia," he extended his hand.

I hesitantly shook it. I was more afraid of him going off on me more, so I figured it would be best to comply.

"I'm Averly Grace," I replied, barely above a whisper.

That aggressive intro turned into a full-blown relationship.

Eight months in, I decided to let him take my virginity. He's the only man I've ever been with, but the things he does to my body make me jolt when I think about it.

Grecia is as hood as they came down to the AK being hidden under the back seats of our cars and under the hood.

He's never home, which was why I wasn't expecting him back so soon tonight.

The only silver lining that gave me peace is that he's not a cheater. I've never dealt with infidelity with him.

I'm not sure if it's because he has integrity or knows my father will kill him.

Grecia is heavy in the streets but not as serious as my daddy. Grecia is a small business, but my father is a corporation. His reach in the streets is longer, and so is his money. That combination allows him to get anybody touched.

Grecia loved the streets. The streets raised him, fed him, and made him a savage.

He wasn't going to let me or anyone else replace his first love.

It's the reason I believe despite him proposing three years ago that we still didn't have a date set.

I wasn't in love with him, but I loved him enough to look towards a future with him. It was his fault that everything was about to go left.

The more I thought about it, the more pissed I became.

"Why are you staring at me?" Grecia asked between breaths of scarfing down his food.

"I haven't seen you in days babe," I ran my hands across his waves.

They were so deep they would make you queasy if you stared at them too long.

"You better put something on your stomach because we are going for round two after this."

"Promise?"

I studied every feature of him, trying to brand it into my memory. I'm going to miss him so much.

"That's a promise."

The pressure between my legs grew just thinking of the sweet love we were about to make.

Once we both were cleaned up after dinner, Grecia came through on his promise.

I kissed him on the forehead before collapsing next to him.

"Did I do something wrong, baby?"

Grecia was still winded from giving me the ride of my life.

"No love, I'm just not feeling well."

"You know I can tell when something is off between us, Grace. Talk to me."

"I'm just feeling sick. I think it's the wine. I overdid it tonight."

"I know what can help you feel better," a devious grin covered his face.

He reached out and bracketed my waist, rubbing the arc of my hip bones with his thumbs.

"Just relax," he lowered his head.

My body sank instantly into the bed; the soft stroke of his tongue enfolded me.

Grecia had a way of pushing every care out of my mind.

*   *   *

"You not about to disrespect me in my house!"

Grecia's yelling jolted me from my peaceful sleep.

"You ain't seen disrespect yet!" I heard my daddy's calm yet deadly voice.

"Oh, God!" I whimpered.

I quickly scrambled out of bed, grabbed my red satin robe from the floor, and booked it downstairs.

I knew whatever was happening was already in full effect, and there was nothing I could do to stop it.

"Daddy!"

He locked eyes with me as he sheathed his blade in the scabbard of his belt.

A fine sheen of sweat shimmered on Grecia's upper lip.

Both of their shirts were decorated in blood and wrinkles.

"Daddy, what are you doing here?"

"Averly Grace Saccone, when I said I would be here at ten in the morning sharp, that's exactly what I meant," his jaws flexed as he spoke.

I cut my eyes to the wall clock in the living room, and it read nine fifty.

"You're early."

"In any event, you nowhere near being ready."

"You don't have to go nowhere with him! I knew something was going on with you last night, and you sat there and lied in my face, Grace! We don't lie to each other! Ever! That's the rule!"

"If I don't, things are going to go sideways, Grecia. I can't allow that to happen."

"Yeah, you're right. If you leave with him, things are going to go left really quick! The rest of Houston may be scared of him, but I'm not!"

My father pulled his Nina out this time.

"Daddy, please!"

"Nigga we can pistol play if you want," Grecia upped his gun as well.

Tears poured from my eyes. I hated that I didn't have time to prepare Grecia for what was about to happen.

I was going to get up early and explain things to him, but he wore me out last night.

I can't let him or my dad get hurt. What my dad had going on was bigger than trying to hold on to a relationship with a man who still has yet to make me his wife after three years.

"I have to do this. I have to go through with this wedding. It's the only way to secure the alliance. If I don't, it's going to be a blood bath in the streets. If you think that doesn't affect you too, then you're crazy!"

"Baby, you don't have to do this. Stop letting this man use you as a pawn. You don't owe him anything. You are not your mother; you don't have to sacrifice your life for him!"

Pop!

"*Arrgghhh*," Grecia screamed as the gun fell from his hand.

"Daddy!"

"It just grazed him. He'll be alright. Don't ever speak on my dead wife again! You find a different way to prove your point."

"Grace, if you leave with him, you'll be sorry."

"Is that a threat?" My dad pulled his gun back out.

"That's a promise! I ain't never been scared of you, and I'm not about to start today. That's why she loves me. I make her feel safe in a way you never could!"

My dad just smiled at him.

"Averly Grace, you can leave your things. You don't need anything you have here."

"Daddy, you need to give me some space! I said I would do it! Some things aren't replaceable," my gaze fell on Grecia, who was nurturing his wound.

"Av-"

"Daddy, if you don't give me this, I will make this whole transition hell for you. I will make it messy and embarrassing to the point no one would want such a wife by their side."

He squinted his eyes in anger, but he knew I could be a handful, so he threw up his hands and walked towards the door.

"You have two hours," he tossed over his shoulder before leaving.

"Let me help you," I kneeled to help him.

"Get off me!"

My head hit the floor when he pushed me off him.

"Have you lost your mind?"

"Have I lost my mind? You about to walk out of here and marry some random nigga, and you asking me am I out of my mind?"

Grecia kneeled over me with his hands tightly wrapped around my neck.

I tried to pull his hands from my throat, but he was too strong.

"Gre-Gre," I choked out.

Just as I was about to lose consciousness, he let my neck go.

"You know how much I love you," his voice was as soft as a feather yet cold as a hungry tomb.

"If you wanted forever, you would've married me by now. It's been three years. The streets come first, and you weren't allowing anyone to replace her. I've been waiting years to buy my gown, plan our wedding, and spend the rest of my life loving you."

"You never wanted to marry me, Averly! Don't you think I could feel you holding back with me? I never pressed it because I felt like you would come around once you realized I wasn't trying to play with your heart. I was in these streets trying to make sure I could give you the life your father swore I couldn't."

"That's not completely true, Grecia. You can't use maintaining a life you had before me as the reason you ran the streets. I was always on the back burner waiting for you to see me. I was always waiting for you to love me properly. When the streets called, you ran. You gave no thought about what you were reinforcing in my heart."

"And what was that?"

"That I only existed when you needed me."

"I guess we both been holding in how we feel about one another. I guess it's not your fault you're a pushover."

I've been told this most of my life. I just wasn't a fan of confrontation. For some reason, Grecia's words rang out louder than they ever have.

"I'm not going to allow you to make me feel like this! You had your chance to make me yours forever, and you chose not to."

"It's whatever at this point, Averly."

"I'm leaving now because I want to. This conversation has illuminated a level of clarity I've been avoiding in this relationship. This argument and conversation just prove that this will never work. I was always in this more than you were. You can't stand my father because you're so much like him. You both just treat me like a piece of property to be utilized at your disposal. I'm not as much of a pushover as you think, Grecia."

"Since we're being honest, I'm glad you're leaving. Being with you was like being in a cage. Constantly having to water down my savage because you act like you couldn't take it. Having to come out the streets to be home with you acting like something I'm not was killing me slowly. A nigga low-key felt like he was on death row."

"Finally...the truth."

I didn't let it show on my face how hurt I was. My heart crumbled into what felt like tiny shards of glass that cut me every time I took a breath.

I walked over to the downstairs closet near the front door and grabbed the bags I packed a few days ago while Grecia was out of town.

I tossed them into the car and drove off. I put Grecia in my rearview and promised never to look back again.

I guess it was a blessing that he conditioned me for the fake love because shortly, it will be my new normal.

CHAPTER TWO

AVERLY GRACE

The Saccone Mansion

Security opened the gate once they noticed my car pulling into the driveway. One section of the gate rolled on a rail to the side, and another could be raised and lowered. I suppressed a shudder once I pulled in front of my father's mansion. It seemed so dark after my mother died. It's now as cold as my father's heart.

My footsteps echoed on the gold-veined marble flooring. My dad's taste was old-world, sumptuous, and expensive, like the authentic tufted Chesterfield sofa that greeted you when you walked in.

Behind elegant banisters, platform walkways permitted catwalk access on the second and third levels. Now I was the one feeling like I was turning myself in for a life sentence with no chance of parole.

"You finally decided to show up," my dad snarked. "I've blocked off the entire south wing for you and your finance. I want you to have privacy while you get acquainted."

My father's words were roaring in my ear. My heart stuttered, and there was this falling, spinning-down feeling.

I stood there bolted in place with every word falling from his lips. I don't know this man or his name. I will be sharing my space with a stranger.

"Fiance? You are really laying it on thick."

I picked my bag up from the floor and decided to head to my room. I agreed not to give my dad problems if he allowed me to come here on my own. I was a woman of my word.

"I can tell you've been settling. Put the bags down. The staff will bring them up to you."

"Whatever," he jerked his foot back when I dropped them at his feet. "What's his name?"

"That's not important. You need to get upstairs and get ready. The esthetician and beautician are waiting upstairs to give you a wax, manicure, pedicure, and do your hair. Do whatever else it is that you do when you're about to spread your legs."

I didn't dignify his response with an answer. I don't know what my dad has going on, but he's never talked to me in this manner.

I didn't snap back at him like I normally do. I just went upstairs to my childhood bedroom to prepare myself for what I was instructed to do.

I don't know the pressing need for me to marry this man, but it made me feel like I had cylinder blocks of cement in my stomach.

My father wouldn't put me in the line of fire, would he?

As far as I knew, the alliance is still in place, so everyone should be at peace. I've been so wrapped up with Grecia that I may have missed something.

My dad and I have been at odds since I hitched my wagon to Grecia's. He didn't trust me enough to keep me in the loop, I'm guessing.

It's too tense right now to ask any questions, so I'll have to figure this out myself.

I stepped out of the shower and admired my body. My reflection was void of life and emotions. I was just a shell of a woman. I have no idea who I am.

For years I've just adapted and been what whoever I was around needed.

I'm always trying to be support beams in other people's lives while mine is tossed by the wayside.

I could faintly hear a knock at the door.

I wrapped my body in a towel before opening it.

"Juanita?"

"So, you're back?"

"I wish on better terms, but yes. I'm back."

Juanita took care of me since I was a little girl. Just knowing she'd be here will make this a tad bit better.

I wonder if she knows what's going on around here with my father?

"Yes, I heard."

"I didn't think you would be here since dad moved you to the summer house."

As Juanita got older, dad transferred her to our summer house because it didn't need as much maintenance.

Juanita and I were always close. My mother died when I was ten. She'd become a mother figure to me. Juanita helped me with my schoolwork, educated me when I started my monthly, and comforted me after experiencing one of the most humiliating nights of my life.

She never tried to replace my mother, but she still cared for me as her own.

I know my dad brought her here to make the transition easier. He wasn't doing it for me, though. He just didn't want me causing problems.

Juanita has always been my favorite. She always will be no matter what.

Being locked in her arms in our embrace was needed. After Grecia and dealing with my dad, I was beyond overwhelmed.

"Let's sit down, baby girl," she patted a space on the bed next to her.

"What's wrong?"

"Your father has gotten himself into some deep doo-doo, my baby."

"What happened?"

"I don't know. All I know is he sent for me to come here six months ago. He's been acting crazy. Constantly mumbling that you're the only way to fix everything."

"I'll find out what is going on."

"Be careful. You may not like the answers to your question, mi amor."

"I know, but you know I won't continue to be blindsided in whatever my father has gotten me into."

"I know. Just please be careful."

"I will. I promise. I need to hurry up and get ready before everyone starts to arrive."

"Okay, I'll send the esthetician in."

"So, you know about that too? Can you believe he set up for me to have a Brazilian wax, Juanita?"

"Yes, I know. That's why I made sure to come and check on you as soon as I got wind that you were here. I'll leave you to it."

"Okay," I hugged her once more before she left.

Whether the answers came from my father or my so-called fiancé, I was going to get to the bottom of my father's erratic behavior.

It took my glam squad over an hour to get me ready. The breeze from the air condition vent had my honey pot feeling like a velvet petal between my legs.

A pile of potential outfits was on my bed. I was going back and forth between the perfect ensemble and the worst one.

Just because I hated the position I was put in didn't mean that I wasn't going to present myself subpar.

I may be a problem, but I'm always the answer.

I decided on a red off-shoulder custom dress I had made a few months ago. It was one of the things I brought with me.

I didn't bother replying to the message from Grecia that he would have my things packed and delivered here sometime within the next week or so.

When I pulled my door open, I could hear male voices near the bottom of the stairs.

I placed my hand on my abdomen to still my nerves. I straightened my back as I headed downstairs. My chest rose and fell with rapid breaths.

My gaze pushed and pulled at all the uncaring faces. My eyes bulged with anger when I locked eyes with him. I was frozen, eyes wide, struggling to comprehend why he would be here?

No amount of time could lapse to make me ever forget him!

My father noticed my expression and knew I was seconds from exploding and making a scene. I may have had my mother's demeanor, but I had his temper, and he knew it!

"This is why you didn't want to tell me because it's him? Oh hell no, I'm not doing this!"

"Get a hold of yourself," my father quivered with outrage.

He grabbed me firmly by my wrist. I could feel my circulation slowing making my hands throb.

Darkness crossed his eyes before he turned around to the rest of the mafia families in attendance, "We'll be right back," he flashed them a fake smile.

His nostrils flared, and his expression grew turbulent as he shoved me into his office.

This was not about to be a pleasant conversation at all.

CHAPTER THREE

LEXINGTON CHARLES

"Are you kidding me right now, LC? You tell me twenty-four hours before you have to go and lay up in some other woman's bed that today is the day?"

Chastity pounded her fist on the wall as she paced back and forth.

"You know how much I love you, but you also know what my family stands for. I have to do what my father asks of me. This request is bigger than me!"

Chastity could care less about how things worked within my family. Although I told her this day would come, she never thought I would walk out the door to build a life with an outsider.

Despite how many times I attempted to explain how things worked in my world, she couldn't grasp the concept. It's one of the reasons my dad said she would never be accepted into our family.

"It's because your dad thinks that I'm not loyal because I didn't grow up in this street life. The faith y'all put behind this fake negro mafia family is delusional! Marrying that Italian slut ain't gone make y'all a legit mafia. They are not going to respect y'all or treat you as equals. Three years of him turning his nose up every time I came around just for you to end it like this? There's nothing you can say that will make me believe you just found out today. Lexington, you giving up your freedom can't be the only way to fix things in your family. There has to be another way, baby! That man is a classic narcissist, and you know that! All he cares about is himself and his agenda. I know that's your daddy, but at some point, you have to stand up to him."

"My father is the only family that I have Chastity, and you know that. Whether I like it or not, I'm next in line to push this legacy forward. I have cousins and uncles, but my dad is my world. You would have to be down to understand the weight the favor of a father carries."

"Here you go with this crap like y'all some type of secret society or something. Y'all ain't no better than anyone else. Just a bunch of hood-rich niggas that had a bit of business sense! Miss me with the bull Lexington Charles! You've never loved me the way you claim!"

"Don't say that because you know it's not true. I've taken backlash from my dad for years due to our relationship."

"And what was the point if all he had to do was snap his finger and you go running? You toss away three years of what we built to run off and appease him. Don't try to come back to me once he's done using you and tossing you to the side like he always does. He treats your cousin Vincent more like a son than you. Why can't he go and marry this trick? He's the one he made sure became a big-time detective. The irony in that."

"That's not how it works. We all have a part to play in this family. My father has worked out every last detail. If I don't marry this girl, he will disown me. I can't allow that because then we would never be safe. Our children wouldn't be safe. That's not a life. You are the only woman I love and will ever love. She will never mean anything to me. I will always despise her for what she will represent."

"What's that?"

"A reminder that I can never be with the one that my heart loves."

"Why don't you just kill him, baby?"

My face was a stiff as a plank of wood. My amazement was hidden by a slow breath that kept me from putting my hands on this woman.

Did she just suggest I kill my father?

"If it were possible, I would've done that by now. It is not for only making me do this but because I love a man who could never love me the same way, Chastity. He looks at me like I'm a constant disappointment. This marriage is the last chance I have to make him proud and solidify my mark in this family."

"You should just be satisfied with having my family surrounding you and me."

"That's not your decision to make. Look, like I said, you knew what this was before either of us caught feelings."

"Exactly, before we caught feelings! I didn't think I would fall in love with you the way that I have. You were so mean I thought we would just smash here and there, and that would be it. That wasn't it though Lexington," she placed her hand on my cheek. "We both entwined ourselves around one another and became one. It was us against the world baby, remember?"

"I remember three years ago you agreed to this as long as we still linked up, and I took care of you. Now the time has come; you're making it impossible for me to leave."

"That's because deep down, I hoped you would finally break free of your toxic father like you did when you told him we were going to be together. I haven't seen that Lexington since that day. I don't know where he went, but I want him back."

"That's because that Lexington paid a price I never spoke on for his rebellion. My father has…ways to punish you other than physically. I'm going to go and stay at my dad's. I don't think staying here the rest of the day is healthy for either of us," I grabbed my bag.

"If you leave out of that door, you better not come back. I won't take you back after this blows up in your face. I'm no one's afterthought. It's all or nothing Lexington Charles."

"I would expect nothing less Chastity. I promise I will love you forever."

Smack!

"Get out!"

My eyes rolled into my head. My teeth gnawed until my bottom lip bled. Walking out of Chastity wasn't as easy as she thought it was.

She had become my peace, biggest supporter, and hype man rolled into one. Something I would never get where I'm going.

As the sting from my face dissipated, so did my humanity. It was necessary to leave my heart with Chasity if I was going to make this believable. If I were going to survive this, I had to become a shell of the man her love attempted to mold.

I loved Chastity, but I wasn't in love with her. At my core, I believed that people use love to manipulate you. This is why I'm able to walk away from Chastity.

My father lived on the other side of Houston, but I needed the long drive to gather my composure.

I knew my father would be looking for any inkling that my breakup with Chasity would be an issue as we advance. I would never put my selfish desires before the family. That's law.

The night I got my brand replayed in my head.

"You will burn in hell like this poker is burning through your flesh if you ever betray this family. Do you pledge your allegiance to the Charles Clan now and forever?"

"Y..eess," I complied through clenched teeth.

I could smell my flesh burning when he lifted the horseshoe, turned halfway to form a "C" on my right shoulder.

Chastity didn't understand that betrayal was not an option in this family.

When I pulled through the security gate, I could hear my father out on his shooting range, letting off rounds. It was his favorite pastime now that he no longer got his hands dirty.

"I'm glad you finally made it, son," he let out a guffaw that echoed throughout the great room.

A flicker of a smile passed my lips. I've never been greeted in such a way by my father. This was already proving to be the right decision. I was grateful that he recognized the sacrifice I was willing to make for our family.

"Was that believable? I'm practicing for tomorrow. I want to make sure I portray myself as a good father to my future in-laws tomorrow."

I went limp. I should've known better. Instantly I made a beeline for the bar to pour myself a glass of bourbon.

I tuned him out as he rambled on and on. He was like a kid in the candy store.

Before the depression, my great-great-grandfather owned a successful funeral parlor back in the 1840s.

Back then, things were still segregated, so black people were able to serve their own communities. Slowly other parlors started to pop up, which sparked competition. When the Great Depression hit, my grandfather's parlor was one of the last ones standing, but he still wasn't making enough money.

We come from a long line of hustlers who were always concocting a scheme, business, or something to generate more money.

My grandfather was very innovative. It was something that has been passed down through the generations. He started bootlegging liquor. His moonshine was one of the best in Texas. He even had the white people buying from him; it was so strong.

Naturally, you make enemies with a growing empire due to jealousy and those just wanting the life you live. My grandfather formed *The Bloody Five*. It started as a handful of people he could trust that he dedicated various business aspects.

One thing those backwood hillbillies could do was make some moonshine, so it spoke volumes that they preferred my grandfather's.

After that, it was bootleg tobacco, opium, then weed. He stayed low and stacked his money. He never did anything flashy or drew attention to himself. He kept his head down until the Dixie Mafia moved into town.

The wars got so bad that they allied. It has been respected and honored for years until The Saccone's took my great-great grandfather's blueprint for *The Blood Five*.

They couldn't push our family completely out because we had roots in the city, but those Italian's didn't make it easy ever since my dad's been obsessed with getting a seat at that table. To take back what he feels rightfully belongs to our family.

"Yeah, tomorrow you will get acquainted with Averly Grace Saccone," my dad casually stated.

The bourbon I was sipping on flew everywhere. I slapped my hand over my mouth not only to dry the liquor I spit everywhere, but I was in shock.

"No, it can't be her," I shook my head defiantly. "Find someone else. I'm not dealing with her."

I followed him inside the house, praying he would listen to my plea.

He marched over to his bookshelf and pulled out one of the drawers to retrieve a stack of papers.

"You will do exactly what you signed off on in this contract! Do you see that? That's your thumbprint in blood! If that doesn't jog your memory, the brand on your right shoulder should!"

"Anyone but her dad!"

"Look, I don't care what happened between you both when y'all were teenagers! Y'all are grown now. Get out of your feelings and, for once, do something to earn the Charles name! You've been off frolicking with that girl for three years, wasting time. Now we're down to the wire. And newsflash, you don't have a choice, so suck it up."

"I don't care how much time has lapsed; we'll never get along, dad."

My dad searched my face as if he were trying to find the right words to say.

He took a seat across from me with his hands clasped.

"It's not that I didn't like Chastity, son. I just didn't want you to end up doing what you're doing now. You had to break her heart because, at the end of the day, it's family first. Your marriage to her would be filled with secrets because she's not built for this life. She would never understand the darkness behind your eyes from the lives you've taken that have stained your soul. Averly Grace was born into this life. She's put family above all others, and that's what's important."

"So this whole time, your issue with Chastity has been that she is an outsider."

"That's it. I think she's a beautiful woman inside and out. She has heart, but we both know that's not enough in this lifestyle. Averly Grace's mother, Elenor, was black. Her father, Neri Saccone, had to get permission from his father, Luca, before marrying her. The only reason they allowed it was because her family had political ties and cops already on the payroll. Marrying her pushed their dynasty forward. Luca eventually died of a stroke. Word is Neri ran the business in the ground because he was consumed with the death of Elenor. Various businesses they owned started getting robbed, they started stealing from within their organization, and other dealers started moving into their territories. It's rumored that Luca put out a contract on Elenor before he died because she was cheating on Neri."

"How did they get paid if he died?"

"The man is a mafia boss. Trust he can get people touched from the grave."

"Did you ever get a chance to know Averly?"

"Not really, she was young. I can't say for sure."

"I hear you dad, but you just don't understand what I went through with that girl."

"I know I don't, but I also don't care. I'm not about to do this back and forth with you. My word is law and what I say goes."

"You have no idea what I've given up for this, for whatever this is."

"This is the only way to make things better between the families. This marriage is the only way to make everyone fall in line. We're the ones getting the better deal. Trust me on that, son. Those greedy Italians have dug themselves in debt, and there's a war brewing. I'm getting what my ancestors started back in blood."

"How are we getting a better deal?"

"Neri Saccone was recently robbed. As I said, they were already down bad. This just made matters worse. He's scared his people are going to put a hit out on him and take his spot."

"Why don't we let them do that?"

"Neri is a fool, but he's an old one. These new cats don't understand mutual respect, and with proper understanding, all parties can eat. When people get greedy, then blood gets spilled. Once blood starts spilling, it's a never-ending war of revenge. I'm not saying we have perfect peace, but we don't live in a constant war zone. Neri's been using his own money to keep their day-to-day operations up and running. He also had to replace what was stolen. People are not trusting him to move their money because he's in a war with who robbed him. No one will front him any money because they don't feel like they'll get it back. He came to me for help to stay afloat."

"What?"

"Yep, imagine that. The proud Neri Saccone coming to me for help. I told him I wouldn't do it just to help him out."

"I don't quite understand, dad."

"The Saccone's may be having money problems now, but soon they will be the top mafia family again. Their blood and connections run deep, son. It's the final piece to push OUR legacy forward. I've been trying to get into that circle for years since they pushed our family out. It was one of my motives for agreeing to the alliance. So, you see, Neri having a daughter and me having you was destiny. I told him that he has a daughter, I have a son. We'll join our houses. Now here we are."

"You mean to tell me I have to sacrifice my life for your plan to come together finally?"

"I'm not happy about this, but it's necessary. The original plan was totally different. Trust me."

"What was it?'

"After the alliance before Luca died, he came to me about an…issue."

"Issue?"

"You can never repeat what I'm about to tell you. Not under any circumstances. I'm disclosing this because it's your right to know. After you marry Averly, you will advance in the rank officially. Not just because of your last name, but now you have sacrifice with it."

"I won't repeat it."

"Neri had a brother named Matteo. Luca found out he was an informant that was causing corruption and snitching to the Feds. Luca asked me to kill him in exchange for him educating me on how a real mob operates. I did it without hesitation. Luca kept his word. He taught me the game while he was alive. It was no secret, and he ain't care how the rest of the families felt about it. Once he died, our organization immediately lost those connections. Neri was too soft to stand ten toes down like his father, Luca. He folded to make the rest of his family comfortable even though he and I didn't have beef. We were pretty cool. It's why he felt comfortable enough to come to ask me for help. Please make this work son so that all of the work I put in was not in vain. In this business, it's always all about who you know. Always," he stressed.

I've never been privy to the entire story. My father is a jerk, so I thought this was nothing more than a power move at my expense.

To find out that this runs more than surface deep changes everything for me. I have to make this work for my dad.

My father has always been a smart businessman. The only that he's been missing is the underworld connections. Not the hood underworld but the real movers and shakers in dark high places.

The Saccone's buried us before we got started, but recompense is on the horizon.

"I got you, dad," I nodded my head as I took another sip of my drink. "At any cost, I will see this through," I assured him.

"I'm relieved you finally understand the depths of this. Come, let's get you something tailored for tomorrow."

"Will Geechie be able to finish it in time?"

"I pay him enough to pull an all-nighter if necessary.

*   *   *

I straightened my suit once we got out of the car when we arrived.

I took a couple of deep breaths and popped a Mentos.

Our driver followed the instructions of the valet. My dad gave Neri instructions that his driver was to be parked as close as possible.

We had so much heat in that car it was crazy. We both had a gun in our side holsters and one on our ankles.

"Son, meet your future father-in-law, Neri Saccone," my father ushered me in his direction.

"A pleasure to finally meet you, sir."

"The feeling is mutual."

I've been in the same circles as Neri but never officially met him.

Neri was clearly anxious. He was talking a lot and moving around constantly. All in all, those from both sides appeared to be getting along for now.

I took the opportunity to familiarize myself with my soon-to-be home. That was part of the agreement as well. I had to live in Neri's home. Supposedly, for him to "get to know me" but it was for him to size me up.

I smiled at the baby pictures of Averly. My stomach dropped when I got to one that looked like she was about seventeen. That was around the time we fell out.

I could tell the picture in the gold frame was her mother because Averly looked like a lighter version of her.

She looked happy as a child. At least one of us was.

My wind got stuck in my throat when Averly came downstairs in that jaw-dropping red dress.

Sweet music leaked into the night as laughter danced between the notes.

It was like she floated down the stairs. She shot me a glare, but there was still a twinkle in her eye.

Yeah, she remembered who I was.

She skewered me with an unflinching look, "This is why you didn't want to tell me because it's him? Oh hell no, I'm not doing this!"

I watched her father grab her firmly by the wrist while he flashed a fake smile attempting to assure us that he could control his unruly daughter.

Same Averly Grace Saccone.

CHAPTER FOUR

AVERLY GRACE

"You promised me you would make this work Averly Grace!"

I could see the veins in his neck pumping the rage through his body.

"Mr. Saccone, we need a moment alone if you don't mind," Lexington interrupted us like he already had papers on me.

"Absolutely."

My father didn't even think twice about leaving me alone with this stranger. He probably couldn't wait to pawn me off on Lexington Charles.

He towered in front of me, standing six foot four. He tousled fro was more tamed than it was wild. His chocolate brown skin and herculean stature couldn't be ignored. His copper-colored skin was flawless, and despite him looking mean, you could see kindness in his eyes.

"Get your hands off me!" I attempted to snatch my arms from him, but his grip was too tight.

He was dragging me towards the back, but we both knew he had no idea where he was going. I guided him to the back porch.

It was pleasantly nice outside. The smell of pine wafted through the air. The stars shined extra bright against the pitch-black sky.

When I spun around to face Lexington, I saw both our fathers watching.

I could tell by the smirks on their faces that they thought we were hitting it off.

"There's no way I would've agreed to this had I known it was you! I would've stayed with…"

"With?"

"None of your business. I would've stayed where I was, is what I meant. I can't believe I'm trapped with you in this hell hole of a mansion."

"You're still melodramatic, I see. Are you ever going to forgive me, Averly? We were just teenagers back then. I can't believe you're still holding on to this."

"I'd rather have my nails snatched off one by one than forgive you."

"It's been more than a decade. Surely you can't still be that bitter."

"Wouldn't you be mad if a girl you were going to lose your virginity to stood you up? Not only stood you up but ghosted you!"

"I had something come up, Averly. I see you think the earth revolves around you." His voice broke low as he uttered the violating words.

He tossed his head from side to side as he chuckled.

"Still an arrogant jerk. Who do you think you are? It was my mother's birthday! Everything that she's missed over the years hit me like a ton of bricks. I was becoming a woman but didn't have my mother to teach me how to be one. I was trying to feel something…anything. I felt like an outcast around the rest of you. I was ugly back then with no boobs or butt," I folded my arms across my chest as if they could hide my vulnerability.

"How did you feel like that? I was only allowed around because of my dad's relationship with your grandfather back in the day. It's more that makes up a woman than boobs and butt too."

I waved off his word like they were mosquitoes. Same disrespectful person, he was back in high school.

My muscles quivered with indignation. How was I going to stay married to him? How could I stomach him day in and day out?

"Everyone at that private school was uppity, stiff, and exploring their sexuality to the fullest. The talk about my father letting everything my grandfather worked for go under had spread like wildfire. I was treated like an infectious disease. You were the only one who showed the slightest kindness or attention, Lexington."

"You always laughed at my corny jokes when we hung out between classes."

"I thought when you hung out with me back then that it was genuine. You offered to tutor me in math. I took note of how you lingered with me longer than you did with the other girls. To me, it only made sense based on how we vibed that I let you be the one to take my virginity."

His emotions flitted across his face.

I turned away to look out over the landscape. I straightened my dress with long, nervous strokes.

"It took me weeks to work up the courage to ask you to be my first. I never thought you would agree, but deep inside, I prayed you would. I wasn't trying to keep you. I only wanted to get it out the way so that I could be slightly experienced for my husband."

"I know. We discussed all the logistics. For you to be unsettled, you were very forward about your intentions back then," he came and stood next to me.

He reached out a hand to brush a lock of long hair away from my face.

"Stop. You promised to keep it a secret and to do that for me. I trusted you with my most sacred treasure only for you to stand me up. It didn't make sense, though. We agreed to meet exactly two Fridays from the day I asked you. You gave me the room key for one of the rooms at your father's hotel across town. You assured me the staff would be discreet and arranged for me to come through the private entrance that V.I.P guest used."

"Let me-"

"No! You won't interrupt me. You will walk through every emotion of that mortifying day with me. You had them decorate the room beautifully. You remembered I told you about my obsession with the bleeding-heart flower."

"How could I forget? You always said it was symbolic of your nature. A person who was said to have a bleeding heart was considered to be dangerously soft-hearted. It's something you said you loved and hated about yourself."

"They're normally found in Asia, so my heart stuttered when I walked in the room and saw a vase filled with them," I quickly removed the tear that escaped my left eye.

"I planned that night to be perfect for you."

"So perfect you never bothered to show. When I saw the care and attention that went into the room, I thought I'd made the right choice. I was relieved that what I discerned about you was spot on. I was giving myself to a perfect gentleman. I still have the note you wrote me. You explained that since it was planned, you wanted it to still be special for me. You told me I deserved the best," I stood there shaking, a low groaning sound bubbled from my mouth.

I was transported back into that moment as my sixteen-year-old self as I relived this. I was determined for Lexington to finally understand after all of these years the pain he caused me.

"It wasn't like that, I swear," Lexington's face was drawn in agony, but not over his own pain.

"How was it then, Lexington? I sat in that room waiting. As the time winded down, I drank glass after glass of the red wine you had them chill. When I finally realized you were a no-show, I called Juanita to come to get me. I made her promise not to tell my dad," I snatched the handkerchief he handing to me so I could dry my tears. "Once I found out you weren't dead, I wanted to kill you myself for what you did to me. I was already battling low self-esteem, missing my mother, and a hopelessly dysfunctional father. I needed that moment with you!"

"I tried to tell you what happened, but you never would hear me out. I hate to admit it, but after a while, I started to enjoy the hateful stares when we were in the same room. Watching you from across the room huffing and puffing whenever I would share the same breathing space as you."

"Because you didn't deserve to breathe the air that I did! I would secretly hope that your opps would bust in the room and shoot you down!"

"Daaanggg, like that?"

"Just like that! If I couldn't trust you, then what makes you think I would trust you now as my husband?"

He brushed his hand across my cheek. Every hair on my scalp stood to attention. Every skin cell tingled, every neuron fired with desire against my will.

My heart pounded hard as he finally came to a halt before me, inches from my face.

"That was the night I found out my mother had cancer, Averly. She was on her death bed. My parents kept it from me. I was going through my teenage crap, so I didn't notice back then that she was sleeping more, losing weight, and smoking a lot of weed," he smiled, but pain covered his eyes like a cataract. "My father wasn't officially a part of the mafia, but he used everything your grandfather taught him to set up his organization on their principles. My mother's funeral seemed like it lasted forever."

"It was the same when my mother died. I was only ten. Soon it was no longer safe to be at home with all of the wars my dad started. We still don't know who killed my mother."

"I'm sorry to hear that. I thought it was a car accident, though?"

"It was made to look that way, but anyway, that's why I think I clung to you back then. I was being pulled into a black hole. You were the light I thought would pull me out."

"There's nothing else that would've stopped me from being there that day. I had a crush on you too. You weren't an ugly duckling to me back then. You were beautiful and authentic. Rare. I never thought you would give me a real chance because I wasn't one of y'all."

I did my best to make sure Lexington couldn't tell that I enjoyed what I was hearing. My face had softened, but he wasn't off the hook completely yet.

"Depending on me then versus now, it a totally different ball game. I'm a man now, Averly Grace. I understand my obligations as such. I understood them back then; however, I lacked the communication skills to express myself. I'm sorry about breaking your heart back then. We're in this now. We might as well clear the air because when it's time to get married, we don't need any uncertainties. Like it or not, our loyalty has to be with one another. We don't know how this is going to play out in the long run. I gave up my life for this."

"So did I," my eyes fell to the concrete as a glimmer of Grecia flashed through my mind. "Did your father tell you how all of this is supposed to work?"

"Not really."

"I suggest we go back inside and find out."

We've both were being thrown into this with no real explanation of what is to be expected. From what I know about Lexington's father, Dasante Charles, he's a piece of work as well.

Lexington secured a firm but gentle lock on my wrist, "Before we do that, I want you to know that I promise to treat you with kindness and be fair to you. I'm hoping now that you know why I didn't make it all those years ago that we can be friends again. I'm not trying to be the boss of you. I know that's what's expected in this culture, but that won't be our life. I don't want to force you to do anything, Averly. I want to be your partner if you let me. This is forced on both ends, but I'm hoping we can make the best of it."

I wasn't sure how to process all of this. I was overwhelmed, but this could've gone all the way left had my father chosen someone else to merge our empire with. At least I knew Lexington, and he was attempting to be nice to me.

I'm pledging my undying affection to him, for now, my wagon was hitched to his. There was no point running it off of a cliff.

"I'm in Lexington."

He smiled as he entwined my hand in his, "At least now it will be more believable."

I mirrored his smile, but deep down, thoughts of Grecia were gnawing away at me.

He acted a plumb fool when I had to leave, but I still missed him.

I couldn't shake him altogether as of yet. I could still feel the quakes of him through my body.

For now, I was helpless. There's nothing I could do concerning Grecia. It's best, for now, to leave well enough alone.

From here on out, I was bound to Lexington Charles forever.

Once we made it back inside, the party had started to thin out a bit. Both families mainly wanted to put their eyes on us to make sure this was really happening.

Members of The Bloody Five were disgusted by my father's decision, but nothing could do about it. He was in charge. To go against him was to go against the family.

"It was nice to see you both getting acquainted," my father sang. "Let's all go to my office."

He was still inelegantly chipper.

My dad took a seat behind his desk. He motioned for Lexington and me to take the seats in front of him. Dasante, Lexington's dad, pulled up a chair so that he was able to see everything going on.

"These are terms of service agreements we all will be signing. You two will be expected to have children together to solidify this alliance and keep the families going. You will need to display public affection so that the community will accept you. If they don't, all of this will be for nothing. This is a very feasible merger. My father was grooming Dasante back in the day before he died. Our community wasn't ready for such a change back then, but I know they are now."

"The wedding is thirty days away," Dasante interjected. "Neri will pay for the wedding as the father of the bride. I will pay for the flowers as the father of the groom."

I rubbed my face with both hands. When I dropped them back onto my knees, they made a slap. My eyes were wide, if not a little manic.

All I could think of is how my wedding was supposed to be with Grecia. I could've done things the way I wanted.

I don't know what this wedding would look like. I shuttered to think of the end result. If I had my way, my wedding would take place in a botanical garden where I could pay to be surrounded by bleeding-heart flowers. I could invite who I wanted, and it would look like a wedding instead of a funeral.

I rose like a wasp had got a hold of me. I sprinted to the bathroom to gain my composure.

I just wished my mama were here to hold me, love me and assure me everything would be okay. I wanted to lay in her lap as I used to while she raked her fingers through my hair. I was so at peace I would drift off to sleep no matter what level of despair I was in.

I never imagined that this would be my life. I know if my mother were still here, it wouldn't be.

I'm not disillusioned about the reality of how things were with Grecia, but he was familiar. I loved him, but we both knew I wasn't in love with him, at least not the way normal peopled loved one another. I still wanted good things to happen for him in his life, just not without me. I was breaking inside without him.

Grecia wasn't perfect, but he was my escape from this life.

"Go away," I whimpered when I heard the soft tap at the door. "Just give me one freaking minute, daddy, to get this out! It's happening too fast. It's all happening too fast!"

I violently pulled the door open when I heard a snicker on the other side of the door and then Lexington Charles' voice.

"I understand that you're not ready because I'm not sure if I am either. But we're partners, remember?"

He squeezed through the crack in the door and closed it behind him. He took a seat next to me on the floor.

"Chastity. That's her name. The first time I stood up to my dad, it was to be with her. She makes me feel like I can walk on water Averly. She's my peace and my storm all at the same time some days. Her smile can make the sunshine break through on the cloudiest of days. I miss her, and I had to break her heart to make this happen for my family."

"Grecia. That's his name. He wasn't perfect, and neither was I, but I chose him. It started as a way to get back at my dad for being so cold once my mother died, but I started to fall for him. As much as I could anyway."

"What does that mean?"

"My dad told me there was no point in getting serious with him because he wasn't one of us. Eventually, I would have to hurt him to do what was best for the family."

"I don't mind if you sneak off to see him from time to time. You just have to be careful. If anyone finds out the logistics of what's really going on, it could start a war."

"I know. I don't mind if you see Chastity either. If you hurt her anyway close to how you did me, then you better think of a grand gesture, my friend," I nudged him.

"There's nothing wrong with making our own side agreements. We can't let our fathers control everything, now can we?"

"No, we can't," I flashed him a smile. "Thank you for listening."

"That's what husbands are for, right?"

"You ain't my husband yet, buddy," I giggled. "Can you help me off the floor in this tight dress, though?"

"I got you."

"I really hope so, Lexington."

"Are you okay, my dear?" My dad asked.

"Yes, I'm fine. We can continue."

"Well, the engagement party will be at the end of this week."

I gave him a skeptical look. He was forcing this alliance through as quickly as possible.

"That's not long enough for us to get reacquainted enough to make it believable to everyone else. We need more time, dad."

"I know you are apprehensive and scared. Other cultures who arrange marriages don't bother with semantics, such as parties or weddings. You should be grateful. I'm allowing you some normalcy through this ordeal."

I was about to take another break, but Lexington grabbed me by the waist, "I'm sure we will be fine."

His dad nodded in approval when he noticed him take control of the situation. So much for not trying to make me do anything I didn't want to do.

I was relieved to finally sign off on the last page of the terms of service.

Lexington leaned in and kissed me on the cheek, "I'll see you tomorrow. I need to get home and rest so I can prepare for this long week ahead of us."

"Oh, you won't be leaving tonight," Neri interrupted us. "You two will need all the time together you can get if this is going to be convincing."

"What?" we sounded off in unison.

"This was perfect planning with Averly's concern about the time and all."

Lexington's angry gaze sliced my face.

"I have the entire wing blocked off for you both."

"I thought that was for me?"

"It's for you both."

"I'm already having your things brought over," Dasante informed Lexington. "You might as well sit back and relax. This will be your home until we can trust you both to live on your own."

"What? Like we're some prisoners?"

"No, like you're a legacy on which the survival of our families is dependent."

"You've made me proud, son. I need to run now."

"Dad, can I speak with you privately before you leave?"

"We will catch up tomorrow, Lexington. I told you that I have to go."

Lexington's fingers covered his mouth as if to hold the scream he wanted to belt out inside. His face soured as he drew his frame from me.

"Welcome to the family, son," my father extended his hand to Lexington, who hesitantly shook it.

"Ridiculous. I need to go unpack."

"I'll go with you."

"If I wanted someone to follow me around, I would've bought a dog!"

He ignored me and kept walking.

"I'm not a dog. You don't have to constantly remind me that you're unhappy because we both know you're not the only one. You might as well quit bucking the system because there's nothing we can do about it," Lexington barked between clenched teeth. "I was cynical at first, but I'm making the best of it. If you're going to remind me how miserable you are constantly, I suggest you keep your mouth shut while I get us through this. Your selfishness is childish," he looked away and delicately pinched the bridge of his nose.

"Selfish? How dare you!"

"How dare I what? Speak the truth! I'm not about to baby you like everyone else in your life. You better grow up, and I mean quick."

I stormed into my bedroom and swirled around so that our nose was almost touching.

"I would give the shirt off my back to anyone who needed it! You have no right to judge me. You don't know me!"

"Giving the shirt off your back to someone isn't the only qualification for not being selfish. You're selfish with how you choose to share your feelings. Just because you feel a certain way doesn't mean you get to let, the words fall out of your mouth any kind of way. You don't know what the other person is dealing with. You swing your words around like boulders. It's not fair to those around you."

"You're supposed to be such a man, so why would little ole' me have you feeling some type of way?"

He shook his head from side to side, "You have so much to learn. I hope you are less of a problem in days to come because if not, then we're in for a long ride."

I can't believe he was sitting here making me out to be the problem like he has risen about all the crap we both have been thrown into.

"This can't be your room?"

His face was turned up like my room didn't meet his quality of living.

"Don't touch my things!" I snatched my ballerina jewelry box my mother gave me for the tenth birthday from him. "What is my room not to your liking?"

"As bad as your attitude is, I thought that you would have a bigger room. You still bunkered down in your room from your teenage years. No wonder you can't move on from the past."

"Well, lucky for you, we have five more in this wing for you to choose from. Take your pick! I always sleep in here when I'm home. I'm short, but I'm not a child so stop playing with me like I'm one."

Lexington towered over me as he mauled over my words. He was an easy six foot four. He was way taller than Grecia, who was six feet even.

Tall men were my type. Being four eleven, it was something about being manhandled by the hulking body of my man.

Not that I wanted that with Lexington. I quickly dismissed the thought of his body on mine.

"What are you staring at?" His gaze locked with mine before I walked away.

"Nothing, I need to get unpacked," I mumbled.

He took a seat on my bed and started to bounce up and down.

"Can you please not do that? Get off my bed! I don't want it smelling like that God-awful cologne you're wearing. Besides, you still have your outside clothes on."

"Outside clothes?"

"Yes, you haven't cleaned up to get into my bed. Those clothes have been lingering in different atmospheres. They're not clean."

"First of all, you're lying. Sauvage by Dior always makes female's mouths water when I'm around. Secondly, you might as well get used to it because it's my signature scent. You will smell it for the rest of your life if this works out as planned. Secondly, my apologies for sitting on your bed in my outside clothes Ms. Saccone."

His words made my stomach tremble and not in a good way.

He had just given me this whole spill about what comes out of my mouth, so I decided it was best to just keep my feelings to myself.

CHAPTER FOUR

LEXINGTON CHARLES

I was relieved to hear the knock at the door. I'd been sitting in silence as Averly angrily unpacked her suitcases and bags.

"Come in," she said.

"Mr. Charles, your bags have arrived."

"Thank you, Juanita," Averly smiled at the older Latino lady.

"Finally," I exhaled.

My bags were neatly sitting at the bottom of the stairs.

"Should I take these up to Ms. Saccone's room?" He asked.

"No, I'll be sleeping in one of the rooms down the half from her."

"William, please take them up to Averly's room. Check with her and see if she wants to choose a larger room since she is now sharing her space with her finance."

Once the man was out of sight, Neri turned to me.

"Your father and I were noticeably clear on our expectations in this arrangement. You are to share a bed in case you missed it. Don't worry; I made sure my daughter waxed everything," he weirdly stressed.

What grown man speaks on his daughter in such a way? It was disgusting. The last thing I wanted to hear was my woman's father telling me he made sure she got waxed.

"Your father mentioned that you're eager to do anything necessary for his approval. He won't be happy to hear that you aren't making the most of this experience. Let me give you a tour. Maybe that will make you a bit more comfortable."

"You need this to go through more than we do!"

"What do you mean?"

"Just what I said. I know this is a sinking ship without my father's money. I'm loyal to my family, and it would be in your best interest to remember that. Yes, I will do what's required of me. No, I ain't no punk. You will not push me around or try to use me like some pawn to do your bidding. I'm here to solidify this alliance by marrying your daughter."

"I'm not your enemy Lexington. My approach was wrong, and I apologize for that. I've been watching you for some time. This is not just some random idea. Yes, I've gotten into a bit of trouble," he looked around paranoid that someone could be listening, "but that doesn't mean I know you're not the best choice for my daughter. I promise I won't try to handle you like your father. We all know you are the engine running the Charles machine."

"Your flattery won't work. I and my father's relationship is just fine," I lied. "Are you going to show me around or what?"

The Saccone mansion was huge. It took us over an hour and a half to cover the grounds.

I paused and took a deep breath once I made it back to Averly's door. I could still see Neri creepily peeking from around the corner at the end of the hall.

"What is this dude on," I mumbled.

Instead of being more intrusive, I knocked on Averly's door just in case she was changing. It was only eight o'clock, and I wasn't sure of her bedtime routine.

"What are you doing here? I thought you were taking one of the other rooms."

"Can I come in?" I forced out a chuckle to put on a show for her dad.

"Did you forget something?" She stood blocking the door.

"No."

She studied my face, "Hold on."

Once she returned, she had her robe on. she stepped to the side and allowed me to enter.

I got a small glimpse of her body when she dropped her robe and crawled back into the bed.

It was petite but tight. Her skin was all the same tone and flawless. I noticed the small stretch marks on her butt cheeks that hung out of her pajama shorts slightly.

"I ran into your father when I went to get my bags. He made it clear that I had to sleep in the same room with you, or he would let my father know I wasn't cooperating."

Averly clicked her tongue as if I were lying.

"Listen, I'm not trying to do this anymore than you are. I figure I chill in here for a few hours, and once everyone is asleep, I'll slip into the room next door. Is it okay if I use your bathroom to get cleaned up?"

"No, trust me, my dad will be expecting that."

"I'll make a pallet on the floor then."

She tossed her eyes so hard to the back of her head I thought they were going to roll on the floor.

I ignored her as I went through my suitcase to find myself something to sleep in.

"You might as well unpack your stuff tomorrow too. I cleared you some space," she sighed.

"Wait, you honestly want us to stay in the small room? We're already not getting along. The last thing we need is to be contained in a smaller space Averly Grace."

"I'm not leaving out of my room Lexington Charles," she mimicked me calling her by her first and middle name.

I just shook my head and went into the bathroom. This woman was absolutely impossible. I was over it. I had a long exhausting day. I didn't have to energy to argue with her anymore.

I took my time in the shower, trying to wash away everything that unfolded today.

I dried my body off with the thick white towel and put on my silk pajamas.

I stroked my head with my hands to get the excess water out of my hair and beard.

I cleaned up behind myself before coming out of the bathroom.

This girl had a sheet, thin blanket, and one pathetic-looking pillow stacked on the floor next to the bed.

"You don't have to be stingy. I thought we bonded when you were in the bathroom earlier?"

"I'm too tired to keep up the charade at this point. The bathroom was cool, but this ain't that," Averly snarked.

"I'm tired too! I shouldn't have to sleep on some scroungy pallet that you didn't even take into consideration how I felt even having to sleep on a floor!"

"Watch your tone, and don't be raising your voice at me nigga!"

"Don't use that word towards me!"

"Or what? Better yet, why not?"

"Because you ain't all black! Italians are known for their derogatory words towards black people."

"My mother was black!"

"And? That doesn't mean anything. As I said, don't say that word to me, ever. I've taken all of the disrespect I can stomach for one day."

"I'm so sick of this! I'm not dark enough to be included with my black heritage and too dark for my Italian side!

I snatched the blanket back on the opposite side of the bed and laid down.

I watched her chest heave up and down as her nostrils flared.

She grabbed the remote control and started flipping through channels.

"I can't sleep with the T.V. on Averly."

"Well, I can't sleep without the background noise, and you're in my bed, so deal with it."

She cut her eyes at me and tossed me a pink eye mask, "Here, this will protect you."

"I'm not the one that needs the protection. You're the one who can't sleep without the T.V."

"Whatever," she scoffed.

I noticed she put her robe back on like I was going to cop a feel.

"You don't have to worry. I'm not going to turn it off when you go to bed. It would help, though, if you turned to something that I like too."

"What do you like?"

"Anything educational or historical. I love national geographic for sure."

She let out a deep sigh, "I never had to worry about this with Grecia."

"Well, you're with me now. This is your new norm."

She held a gaze with me for a moment before looking away without a word. She sucked her teeth as scrolled through the guide until she found the history channel.

Accepting the glaring anger that poured from her eyes, I kept my arms folded across my chest. Inside I was laughing. She wasn't used to not getting her way.

I was so drained I could already feel the weight of the pressure of my new life on my eyelids. I could feel myself drifting off. I hoped that Averly didn't kick me on the floor out of spite because I wasn't in the mood.

*   *   *

My internal clock was set to four in the morning. I was astonished that I woke up still in bed. I was sure that Averly was going to push me on the floor. When I rolled over, she was still sound asleep with the remote in her hand.

Her scary butt thought I was going to turn the T.V. off once she was asleep.

She was talking all that smack like she was furious. Who knows, maybe she was. I watched the little demon recharge herself. She would soon be powered up to put the cables on me once she was awake.

I decided to continue with my morning routine before she woke up.

I kneeled in front of the chair near the window and said my morning prayer. As soon as my feet touched the floor, I talked to God before I started my day.

I've done many things that I wasn't proud of. I had faith that God understood the predicament that I was born into.

Once I was done, I took another shower. I loved to start my day fresh. I don't care if I took a bath last night. Today was a new day.

I took my time down the dark corridor. This mansion felt medieval with all the dark hallways. My staff had everything prepared before my feet hit the floor. I expected nothing less here.

I was instantly disappointed when I walked into the kitchen.

The lady Averly called Juanita was just getting things started. The crow's feet near her eyes exposed her seasoned age along with a few strands of silver hair. She looked as if she could use some help.

"Good morning Mr. Charles. Would you like a cup of coffee?"

"Yes, please."

She poured the strongly brewed beverage into a white cup with gold trim.

"Your father's staff sent over a list of things your allergic to and hate," she slid over the printed-out email to me.

I went over it, and everything was there.

"Once you memorize this, can you destroy it?"

"I will be the only one preparing your meals. I've memorized it. Now that you confirmed everything, I can destroy it."

I watched Juanita walk over to the stove. She waved the rolled-up paper over the fire. Once the flames nearly reached her finger, she dropped it in the sink and ran water on it.

She took a paper towel and cleaned the sink out.

I sipped on my coffee as she prepared breakfast.

"Can I offer some unsolicited advice?"

I knew that those who provided service in the house always have the inside track.

"Please."

"Be patient. I know what happened between you both back in the day. I know how deeply you standing her up cut her. That girl can hold a grudge *mi amor* like no other. Be patient with her but be assertive. That girl needs a man that knows how to handle her. She has to trust you, though. She has to know that you only want the best for her."

"I understand. Thank you for your help."

"I'll help you as much as I can. Why don't you take her breakfast in bed? Once I'm done, I'll set it up pretty on the tray for you. That way, you can kill two birds with one stone. If you both enjoy breakfast upstairs, you can avoid Mr. Saccone."

I chuckled, "Is it that obvious?"

"He can be pretty intense. He wasn't always like this. He was different when his wife was alive. A part of him died with her. Averly is similar to her mom in various ways. If he comes looking for you two, I will vouch for you. He will be happy to know you both are taking the time to get to know one another."

"Can I be honest with you about something?"

"Sure," she came and sat at the table near me.

"Before I came here, I had to end it with my woman. We were together for a long time. I cut her off abruptly when my father told me it was time to solidify the alliance. I want to get to know Averly; however, I can't stop thinking about Chastity. That's her name."

"You and Averly are both working through the same thing. She would never admit it, but Averly is in love with Grecia more than she cares to admit. You both have ties to sever if you're going to make this work. There's no way you can stand together if your hearts are divided." She reached for my hand. I placed them in hers while taking solace in her advice. "Sometimes love feels so good because it's forbidden. Trust me, I know! Both of you were with people your fathers didn't care for. You can't deny the chemistry between you and Averly. Who's to say this isn't the forever love you both truly long for? If either of you were with your soul mates, there would be nothing but death that could separate you from them."

"I hear you, Juanita, but I'm not so sure. Averly is a firecracker. She hasn't let up on me since I've been here."

"Just give it some time and effort. You'll be surprised by what can happen if you put a little time on something."

"I will do my best, Juanita. Thank you."

"Your welcome."

She went back to preparing breakfast while I decided to send Chastity a quick message.

I texted that I loved her and hoped to see her soon, but I knew I was blocked when my message turned green.

I can't believe her! She said she wouldn't make this hard and that we could make this work as long as I took care of her.

I was hoping she would stick to what she originally told me. I already knew it was a slim chance of that happening.

As Juanita said, I need to make this work with Averly. I'm just not sure if she's willing to do the same.

Juanita plated everything like was she was a contender on *Master Chef* with Gordon Ramsey. I was pleasantly surprised.

"Here you go," she slid the tray over to me. "You're all set."

"Thank you again for this," I smiled, clutching the tray.

"It's no problem."

I stopped and placed the tray on the table where a fresh bouquet of red roses was on the way back upstairs.

I pull two from the vase and place them on my tray. I always have to add my touch to everything.

I positioned the tray on the table near the window in her bedroom.

Even sleep Averly was attractive. I caressed her velvety skin with my finger. She started to stir slightly.

I took a seat next to her, "Averly," I muttered.

"Huh?" She slowly batted her eyes as she wiped the drool from her mouth.

She cut her eyes at me to see if I noticed, "It's okay," I reassured her. "You're still breathtaking to me."

"I'm pretty sure you have to say that since you're about to be my husband."

"No, I don't, but you're welcome."

"I'm not about to sit across from you with a crusty face and funky breath. Let me go wash my hands and freshen up."

"Okay, I'll be waiting."

When Averly emerged from the bathroom, her hair was pulled back in a ponytail. If I wasn't mistaken, she had on a bit of make-up.

I laughed to myself. This woman was something else.

She joined me at the table and started eating like she was starving. I was glad that she wasn't shy about eating in front of me, though.

"You must've fallen asleep watching T.V. because when I woke up, you were asleep sitting up still gripping that remote control for dear life."

"Yeah, I found something that I liked, which was remarkable. I was going to change it once you fell asleep, but I have to admit I was intrigued."

"It's amazing what we learn about ourselves when we are open to trying new things."

"Mind your business, and I'll mind mine," she snapped.

She wasn't giving me any leeway.

I nodded my head in agreement. It was too early to be trying to argue with her. I was still feeling some type away about Chastity blocking me.

Every time Averly rejected me, it only made me think of Chastity more.

"I won't be able to spend time with you today?"

"Why not? You know our parents are adamant about us getting to know each other. It's going to take both of us to make that happen."

"Chill. I have a standing appointment. My dad knows all about it."

"What? Do you see a therapist? I'm all for protecting your mental health."

"No, and it's none of your business."

"Look, you're not about to keep gaslighting me. We're about to be married. Your business is my business, and my business is your business. There's no way around it, Averly. Stop being so difficult when you know there is nothing either of us can do about this situation."

She just kept chewing her food as if I hadn't said a word.

After a long pause, she finally spoke up, "The gun range. Every month, once a month, that's my time to unwind and recalibrate. I go off to the gun range, and it couldn't have come at a better time," she scoffed.

I nodded my head in agreement. Finally, something I can agree with.

"I'm coming with you. I'm not asking you either. I'm telling you that I'm coming. I'll go and change my clothes in the other room so you can get ready in peace."

She opened her mouth like she was about to protest, but I stood up and left her there. I chuckled under my breath, just seeing her stuck from how I laid down the law.

After about thirty minutes, I heard her door slam shut and her feet moving quickly against the hardwood floors.

She's trying to get away from me. I didn't bother to go after her because this was a lesson she needed to learn in the door.

She's going to learn that if I want to find her anywhere on this earth, I'm able to do just that.

I went into her bedroom and grabbed the breakfast tray. I was glad to see she at least stacked our dirty dishes back on the tray.

"Where should I sit this Juanita?" I questioned her.

"I'll take it," she reached for the tray. "How did it go?"

I just rolled my eyes, "Did you see her high tail it out of here just now?"

Juanita laughed, "Yeah, she can be difficult at times."

"Do you know the name of the gun range she goes to?"

"Full Armor Gun Range."

"Thank you."

"No problem," she smiled before going back to prepping lunch. "The keys are hanging in the garage. They're labeled with the car information. Take anyone you choose."

"Thank you, Juanita."

I went out to the garage and opted for the Maserati. It purred like a kitten when I started it.

When I finally made it, I saw one of the cars from Averly's dad's garage parked out front. I was relieved she didn't lie.

We both admitted to being hung up on our exes. I thought she was plotting to be reckless.

I couldn't wait to get inside to let her know she couldn't get away from me if she tried.

I stopped dead in my tracks when I saw some nigga hissing in her ear. He had his hands gripped around her waist.

I can't lie. I was envious. I could feel the blood rushing through my head. My hands dropped to my sides to form clenched fists of tension. I bet a stack that's that nigga Grecia.

At least she could get him to talk to her. Chastity cut me off with the quickness with no remorse.

Maybe I should pop up on her like this dude did Averly.

I was already starting to regret making that deal with her to still link with our exes as long as we were careful. I've always liked Averly, but we just never could link to see if it could be more.

As teenagers, she was more like a best friend. We talked about any and everything. There was always this underlying chemistry. When she trusted me to take her virginity, I was honored. I did everything in my power to make it special except show up.

I decided to sit back and let her have her fun. I don't do well with rejection, so if she tried to play me, it would be up there.

I scanned the room to see if someone was there that could've taken what was going down back to her father. I don't put anything past that man. I wouldn't be surprised if he wanted to hold a flashlight once we started trying to conceive.

Against my better judgment, I decided to break up her lil' rendezvous.

"Thank you for helping my fiancé, but I can take it from here," I positioned myself between them.

Averly met my unrelenting stare. Grecia, on the other hand, looked like he was ready to bang. I was hoping they didn't jump me. It could go either way at this point with Averly Grace.

She already said our talk in the bathroom was fake. She was just putting on.

It's been a minute since I got my hands dirty, but I could use a refresher. These hands graduated magna cum laude from the school of hard knocks. I could handle any action coming my way.

"Calm down," she placed her hand on his chest to soothe him. "I'll be right back," she told him. "Lexington, can I speak to you outside?" She said through gritted teeth.

I did as she asked to avoid making a scene. The last thing I needed was for her father to tell my dad I couldn't handle myself and brought unnecessary attention to the family.

"You have no right barging in here acting as you own me! We agreed to this, remember?"

"I know, but that's a bad idea now that I see you out in public. Your father could have someone following us! Anyone from the community could've caught you out here with this nigga Averly! You're not about to drag me down with you making these poor reckless decisions! The last thing you need is for the community to label you as a whore or a slut!"

Smack!

I scooped her up and tossed her over my shoulder. I rounded the car and folded her up on the passenger side.

"Put me down," she screamed, beating me across my back and bucking like a wild bull.

"I'm not about to let you make both of us look like idiots. I'm not about to be out here looking like I can't control my woman!"

"I'm not your woman!"

"Right, you about to be my wife!"

I could see Grecia standing on the steps as we pulled off. The right corner of my mouth turned up in satisfaction. *Yeah nigga, it's a new sheriff in town.*

"It's this what it's going to be like with you? You said you weren't going to try and control me!"

"Well, it looks like you need a bit of control to protect you from yourself."

"You are such a hypocrite!"

"Call me what you want, but you will not make me lose everything my family has worked for. You may not care about humiliating your family, but I do!"

"Whatever."

We swerved to the right as the back end of the car fishtailed until it gained control.

She hopped out of the car so fast I could barely shove the gear into park.

"Can you go to the gun range and get the car she drove?" I instructed one of the members of the security team.

"How did he get through the gate?" I mumbled to myself when Grecia sped up behind us.

"Nigga I don't know who you think you are but don't put your hands on my woman! Ever!" He pointed his pistol in my face.

"Grecia, put the gun away," Averly yelled frantically, struggling to calm him down.

"Stay out of this," I warned her.

"Averly Grace go inside," Neri instructed her.

I didn't need him to help me fight my battles. How would I ever get Averly to respect me and know that I can handle myself if he keeps trying to control the narrative?

"But daddy I-"

"Averly Grace Saccone, do as your father asked you," I spat the words out through gritted teeth. Frustration and disdain were wrapped up in my instruction.

They all were about to find out that ain't nothing soft about me.

She narrowed her eyes but did as I instructed of her.

Once she was inside, I turned back to Grecia, who still had his pistol on me.

"This is nothing personal. I know for a fact Averly and Neri told you what was about to go down. What you had with my fiancé is over."

"Yeah, and I know this all is a show."

"Far from a show. Did she tell you how close we were back in the day?"

His face twisted in confusion.

"Based on your expression, I gather that she didn't. I'm not just some random dude who popped up in her life. This was in works long before you."

"Nigga, what's to stop me from pulling this trigger right now for the way you've tried to handle Averly and me?"

"The fact that I know where your family is and I have no issues with paying them a visit…personally," I threatened. "As a matter of fact, your granny has become quite close to her new next-door neighbor Junk Yard."

"Nigga, you cap!"

I snatched my phone from my pocket and called Junk Yard, "Wassup boss man," he picked up on the first ring.

"You near Ms. Bernice?" I asked him.

"Yeah, she is coming out of the house now. I was cutting her grass for her."

"Look at that, can you put her on the phone? Her grandson thinks I'm playin' with him about my new fiancé," I told him.

"We can't have that. Do you need me to make a point?"

"Not this time. I just want to say, hey, for now," I put the phone on speaker so Grecia could hear his precious granny unprotected with the most ruthless killer I know.

"Hello," she sang. I could tell she was smiling through the phone.

"Ms. Bernice, I'm Junk Yard's brother Lex. Now he's been raving about your sweet potato pie. I told him I needed to pay you to make me one," I chuckled.

"You don't have to pay me, baby. I'll send you one next time I make one."

"I sure would appreciate it. Can you let Junk Yard know I had to go? I'll call him later."

"I sure will," she disconnected the call.

"Nigga, I should pull this trigger right now!"

"Yeah, if I don't call my boy back in the next five minutes, he gone blow your granny top back. He sick in the head, so he calls them frontals," I yawned. "I wake up every day expecting to die. You are not scaring me. Pull the trigger or get off my property," I barked.

"I don't take too kindly to threats," Grecia grunted.

"I can guarantee you a threat from Lexington Charles is a promise, and I would be more than happy to make good on said promise," I told him.

I have no idea why I had an attitude or exactly when I became so possessive of Averly, but I was standing on it.

I could be selfish right now. Chastity icing me out could be forcing me more to Averly. Something about seeing him with her igniting something in me that I thought was dead in the past.

"Both of you niggas gone have to see me, and that's on, period!" Grecia jammed the car into gear and gunned the engine.

We watched him speed off after his idle threats. Junk Yard didn't live next door to her, but he always kept eyes on her.

"I'm proud of how you handled that," Neri smiled proudly.

"You need to mind your business. I didn't need your help. You will find out soon enough that I'm more than capable of handling myself, Mr. Saccone."

I stormed past him so I could check on Averly.

When I got up to her bedroom, she was lying across her bed. Juanita was comforting her, who was giving me the stank eye.

"I didn't tell you where she was so you could ruin her day and humiliate her!" Juanita snapped, throwing the dish towel at me before leaving the room.

Once she closed the door, I pulled a chair near the bed to face Averly.

"You're just like all of them. Just like my father, your father, and the rest of the men in the mafia. That's the reason I was with Grecia."

"He's still a thug too. He's just not affiliated."

"I'm not your property or possession. Since you can't remember the promise you made me, I figure I will remind you!"

"I'm sorry things went this far today. I wasn't trying to make you feel like a possession."

"Sorry, won't work. This shouldn't have gone this far, Lexington. I should've had the backbone to leave when Grecia popped up on me, but I didn't. You just ruined everything I had left with him!"

"What? You just sat there and said that you didn't have the backbone to leave, but you want to blame me for checking it? I'm doing the right thing, which is something you fail to see right now! Those contracts were not just a piece of paper, Averly! You are moving like you a little girl, and you're not! This is serious! If either side finds out what we're up to, not only our lives but our father's lives are on the line! I wasn't calling you a whore. I was trying to get you to understand what other people might say if you aren't careful. Who knows how someone would feel from the community if they saw you?"

"That's a big IF Lexington!"

"You just don't get it, do you? Whether we like each other or not, we are bound together. We have a duty to one another! I'm sorry for agreeing to let you see Grecia and then reneging. I have to do whatever it takes for this to work. You may not want to admit it right now, but you know how dangerous it was for you to be in public with that nigga."

"His name is Grecia."

"Whatever."

"You just don't get it!" She yelled.

"I get that you're a selfish brat who never had to do anything for anyone else but herself! I understand that when you don't get your way, you will hurt anyone until you do! I won't keep trying to be your friend. It's clear that the only thing you understand is being treated as property. If I have to be like my father or yours to have a successful marriage, that's what I'll do," I stormed out the door.

My heart sank when I heard her sobbing on the other side of the door, but I refused to fold. Averly had to learn that her loyalty was to me whether she wanted to pledge it or not.

CHAPTER FIVE

LEXINGTON CHARLES

I picked over the honey-glazed grilled salmon that Juanita prepared. Everything from the homemade mashed potatoes to the broccolini was plated beautifully. I was still frustrated with Averly's behavior. I've always known she was a brat, but her behavior today was inexcusable. I partially blamed myself for telling her that I was cool with her still seeing Grecia, but I had no idea that she would be so reckless.

I snatched my plate up so I could go up to my bedroom and eat. The last thing I needed was Neri telling me how I should handle my wife and marriage.

He needed to understand quickly that his daughter will soon be my primary responsibility. I'm not tolerating him thinking he about to run anything in my home.

I can't wait until our probationary period is up after we get married. Once our parents are sure we understand the ramifications of going against the contract, we'll be cleared to move into our place.

When I got to the top of the stairs, I just stared at her door. It's beyond me why she acts like she doesn't understand what's at stake here.

I rotated my head from side to side and went into my bedroom. I fought the urge to be the peacemaker this time. I wasn't wrong. She was.

I'm always the one trying to smooth things over and explain. I'm not doing that this time. I'm done being the nice guy. She doesn't understand anything but dominance and control.

I never wanted to be that to her because something tells me that has been her life with her daddy. I figured that since we were both put into a predicament beyond our control, we had some sort of bond and understanding. I was wrong.

I found more peace in the comfort of the bedroom I was still getting used to. I was able to finish my dinner as I read the newspaper. Someone is going around robbing businesses downtown. Not just randomly either. All the owners were in the life. Whoever it was had to be pretty bold to pull off such a move.

When I pulled the door open to take my plate back downstairs, I ran into Juanita.

"I'm sorry. I didn't mean to startle you. I apologize for how I reacted earlier. I'm very protective of Averly. She's like a daughter to me."

"I picked up on that much, and I understand. I was acting in Averly's best interest. We both know what would've happened if someone in the community would've seen her."

She nodded in understanding, "Just be patient with her. She will come around. I promise."

"I'm not so sure about that. Averly hates my guts."

"Trust me, and whether she admits it or not, she knows you did the right thing. You're right. There is a tremendous amount on the line right now."

"Thank you."

I managed to make it downstairs and back without bumping into Neri.

I wasn't known for dodging any action, but I preferred to move smart right now. I was still feeling out my surroundings and the people in it.

I preferred sitting back and watching people, places, and things. You can learn more from a person by just watching them or listening to them talk.

A person who's always bumping their gums isn't absorbing much information.

I put my hand under the faucet to measure the temperature of the water before turning on the shower.

The white marble had gold cracks scattered throughout. The showerhead matched, but the gold sparkled more as spatters of water covered it.

I let the water wash over me. I just wanted to be home with Chastity. I missed showering with her. The way the water would trickle down her spine to the dip in her back.

My manhood jumped just thinking about that woman. I wasn't counting on getting any action from Averly anytime soon. I wouldn't be a man if I didn't admit that the thought of being intimate with her didn't cross my mind. In the meantime, I had to concentrate on keeping both of our families alive since she refused to.

I sighed under the hot water wishing I could follow it down the drain. I hated it here. I felt like I was in a minimum-security federal prison with no chance of parole.

My skin started to wrinkle under the now lukewarm water letting me know it was time to get out. I ran my hand across my waves to remove the excess water. I wrapped the towel around my waist and grabbed my dirty clothes.

I kept forgetting to ask Juanita who handles the dry cleaning. For the time being, I just put everything in the wicker basket in the corner.

I cast the slightest of glances at Averly sitting on my bed before focusing back on disposing of my dirty clothes.

"You're so arrogant," she snorted with derision.

"It's called confidence, and you're worried about the wrong thing. Did you come to apologize?"

"What do you mean? I wanted to allow you to apologize to me!"

She hissed like a cornered serpent ready to strike its victim.

"Look, I'm not about to argue with you. If you came in here to get loud and make a scene like a bully on the playground, then I would rather you just leave."

"Leave? This is my daddy's house, need I remind you. You don't come up in here giving me orders. I can go and do as I please up in here!"

"You're acting like a child, as usual. When are you going to grow up? Not just our lives but our family's lives are on the line. You're stomping around this room yet to grasp the bigger picture of what we're facing if this doesn't work! You know what?"

I wasn't going to go back and forth with her. I picked her up and tossed her over my shoulder.

"What are you doing? Put me down!"

She pounded her fist against my back, but it didn't do any good. Those hits felt like a Russian massage, which I needed with all the stress I was carrying.

She treated me with a look of unmitigated fury. It was the last thing I saw before closing my door in her face.

Every insult she hurled emerged accompanied with a groan. I put on my boxer briefs while she continued making a fool of herself in the hallway.

Suddenly, it stopped. I could hear mumbling on the other side of the door. I pressed my ear against it. It was Juanita.

"Stop it! You calm down, Ms. Lady! You don't act like that! You know better!"

I gave a little whisk of a smile and continued listening. I was glad to have at least one person who was neutral for the most part. Juanita seemed to be a fair woman. I can dig that.

I quietly cracked the door. I wanted a visual so I could hear better.

"I know you're frustrated, *Mami,* but you have to make this work. You shouldn't have agreed to something you wouldn't commit to wholeheartedly," Juanita continued.

"I didn't agree to this, Juanita," she whined. "He's making me do this like he made me major in accounting and business. Like he made me stay under a certain weight when I was just a teenager! Like he made me have these stupid implants! I never wanted any of this! I just wanted my mama! If she were here, none of it would've ever happened! I still don't know where he had her buried! What is the big secret?" She broke down.

"Now, now *hija.* It's okay," Juanita embraced Averly. "I don't agree with how Mr. Charles dragged you out of the gun range, but you know he did the right thing. This agreement is still new. Anyone could be watching you two. You didn't even bother to go somewhere private, Averly. This is not a game. They will kill your entire family to wear the crown."

"You're all against me. No one understands how I feel!"

"That's why I've always felt like you needed siblings. You are self-absorbed because you never had to worry about anyone but yourself. Your father iced you out a long time ago. You've just been trudging along in life. Have you thought about how Mr. Charles feels? He's in a house that doesn't belong to him with people who don't care for him. He's the one most alone in this right now. You have me to lean on. Who does he have?"

"I didn't think about it like that, Juanita. You know you're pretty much the only one who can reason with me. I will try harder. I know I can be self-centered, but you're right. Lexington has to be feeling so alone."

"I saw him bring you breakfast in bed. He's trying to make the best of the situation you both are in. I'll take you at your word that you will make this right."

Juanita hugged her once more, and Averly walked into her bedroom.

I felt a bit of relief that Juanita was able to reason with her. Only time will tell if she listened or not. We've both been forced into this situation. There's no point in us making this life we must build on a lie, a living hell.

I closed my door a got in bed. I surfed through the channels until I found something on the History Channel that caught my attention.

Thirty minutes into my show, I heard a light tapping on the door.

"Who is it?"

"It's me, Averly."

My door wasn't locked, but I still got up to greet her.

"What can I do for you, Ms. Averly Grace?"

"I would like to talk to you. Not yell, just talk."

"What's going on, Ms. Saccone?"

"I just wanted to apologize for my behavior. I've never had to see anyone else's perspective but my own. I'm sorry, I didn't mean for things to go left like this. I never thought about how all of this was affecting you."

"I understand. We just have to be more patient with one another. If this is going to work, we have to get to know one another the best way we can."

"Have you heard from Chastity?"

"No, she cut me off completely. That's not why I pulled you out of the gun range, though. We don't know who's watching us. I'm just trying to keep us safe."

"I know. This whole situation just upsets me. It's just another thing my father has forced on me. No shade."

"None was taken. I'll get my things so I can come to sleep in your room," I told Averly.

"We can sleep in here tonight. We can rotate until we find out what works. This room is way bigger than mine, so who knows."

"Yeah, but your bed is way more comfortable," I laugh quietly.

I wasn't sure why Averly was so nice other than Juanita's pep talk. I don't know how long it was going to last, but I better enjoy it.

Averly hopped on the other side of the bed like a kid. I smiled and laid next to her.

"If you don't sleep with the T.V. on, what do you normally do at night?"

"Just pray and go to sleep. Since I've been here, I watch a little because I'm not used to not sleeping in my bed. I can't let my guard down because I don't know what to expect."

"We have security. Nothing is going to happen to you here."

"You know the life that we're in. Things can change in the twinkling of an eye. Besides, this is not my home. I'm a guest here. This arrangement could go left at any given moment."

"I understand. So, you pray, huh?"

"Yeah."

"I don't remember the last time I prayed."

"It's easy for life to consume you and make you feel like you have to solve everything on your own. It's easy to feel you're on your own when your life is so out of control, but prayer helps me. I can pray with you anytime you want."

I could see Averly blush. She just nodded.

Averly tossed around in the bed a bit, trying to get comfortable.

"Here, try this," I handed her a pillow so she could prop herself up. "You don't have to watch this if you don't want to. We can watch something you like."

"No, we can watch this."

"Good, the Vikings, come on tonight. If you like it, maybe we can go back, and binge watch it so you can catch up."

"Deal," she smiled.

Every now and again, my eyes would go to Averly, whose eyes were glued to the T.V. She was immersed in the show.

"So, what did you think?" I asked her once the show had ended.

"I love it! It's a bit bloody and gruesome, though."

"It's not different than what we do daily," I told her.

"Who? My day-to-day activities are not like that. I handle the meetings, scheduling of transports, and finances. Now don't get it twisted; I will bust if necessary," she smirked.

It was kind of sexy that she seemed so fragile but had a beast that resided within her.

"Well, if I have to get involved, it's bad, and I pray you never have to see that side of me. I'm laid back and unproblematic, but Averly, I promise with me you are safe."

She slid a curious glance my way as she bit down on her bottom lip.

Our attention went to the thick wooden door when we heard a knock from the other side.

"Who is it?" Averly asked.

"It's dad," Neri replied.

Averly pulled the covers up to her chest and moved closer under me.

The corners of my lips quirked into a light smile.

"Come in," I replied.

"Sorry to interrupt you two, but we have a meeting tomorrow. Lexington, I need to make sure we can work well together."

"I'll be ready," I assured him.

"Well, I'll take my leave. Enjoy your night," he said.

"Let me do the talking tomorrow."

"I'm not useless, Averly. Your dad wants to get a feel for how I do business. He wants to know if he can trust me not to mishandle his empire."

"Please let me take the lead on this one," she rebutted.

"I have no problem with my woman leading as long as she's leading us to greatness. I would enjoy seeing you in action. It will give me a feel for how you move in business. Your father will have plenty of opportunities to see how I navigate the time comes. You can handle it tomorrow. I have your back though," I turned off the light and handed her the remote control.

I could tell she appreciated the gesture. She gave me this goofy smile as she took it from me.

We didn't have the tension in the room we had last night. Averly was still tucked under me.

Her soft skin felt nice next to mine. She smelled like coconut and some other flowery scent I couldn't quite place.

CHAPTER SIX

AVERLY GRACE

I slept like a baby in the bed with Lexington. The first night was uncomfortable and awkward, but it wasn't like that this time. I didn't feel the need to cover myself up in my nightclothes or sleep with one eye open. It just felt right.

When I rolled over, Lexington was on his knees praying. I didn't want to disturb him, so I just watched silently.

I hurried and closed my eyes when he started to shuffle like he was about to get up. I felt like a creep watching him.

I could feel him looking at me even with my eyes closed. He gently pulled the blanket over my shoulders before he went into the bathroom.

When I heard the shower come on, I jumped out of bed and went to my bedroom to get dressed.

I wanted us to go downstairs together. I rushed to pull one of my power suits from the closet. I took a quick shower to freshen up. I gathered myself together and pulled my hair into a high bun. The matte red lipstick made my lips pop.

"Wow," Lexington's body came to attention when I stepped into the hallway. "You are stunning."

"Thank you," scarlet heat caressed my cheeks. "Why are you always gassing me up?"

"I'm telling the truth."

"Yeah, you are," I laughed.

Knowing that Lexington was not the cold-hearted snake I thought he was made me view him differently.

He extended his hand, and I politely accepted. We descended the staircase as a loving couple. Something I knew my dad would be glad to see.

"Good, you both are ready. I can bring you up to speed over breakfast."

Lexington pulled out my chair. I released a single button at my waist so I could take a seat. Juanita was in the kitchen grinning from ear to ear.

I poured us both a cup of coffee.

"I drink mine black," Lexington educated me.

"So, do I," I smiled.

"We'll be meeting with Giovanni, who keeps complaining that he wants out. I've disregarded his complaints, but now he's starting to mummer to others in the community. I haven't killed him because we're already bringing the Charles' into the fold. I don't want to cause any more waves for now. I want their respect. I fear that my age gives the impression that I will no longer slaughter an entire family if necessary to get my point across. Instead of traveling down that road, I would like first to try and send in younger leadership. Maybe you two can ignite a flame that will help him see the light."

"I'm sure we can come up with something. When we show up together, that will also show Giovanni that additional strength and power have been added to the empire. I'm sure he'll be eager to prove his worth. I'll let Averly take the lead since he's familiar with her," he placed his hand over mine when he was done speaking.

I didn't flinch this time like before. Instead, it felt like butterflies filled my stomach. I could feel the heat in my cheeks. I silently prayed that Lexington or my dad wouldn't notice me blushing.

"That would be a great idea. Lexington, you are free to act in the full power of your authority as long as no one dies. This merger is still fresh. The last thing we need is an internal war."

"Understood," Lexington nodded in agreement.

"We need to get going if we don't want to be late," I tipped my head in Lexington's direction.

Approval gleamed in my father's eyes. I could tell he admired the fact that Lexington and I were getting along.

The car was already waiting for us once we were outside. The chauffeur took three ground-eating steps to open the car door.

"Hello, my name is Lexington Charles," he extended his hand to the driver. "And you are?"

"Amos, sir," he firmly gripped Lexington's hand.

"When she's with me, you don't need to open her door. It's a privilege I don't take lightly."

"Understood, sir."

I drifted toward him like smoke when he extended his hand to help me into the car.

I slid over so he could get in. His YSL cologne assaulted my nostrils seductively. He's never worn that one before since he's been here.

We vibed out to the classical version of *Girls Like You* by *Maroon Five*. I told Amos to play it whenever I got in the car. Ever since *Bridgerton* aired on Netflix, I've been obsessed with the soundtrack.

The violin's sweet sound leaked into the atmosphere of the car as joy danced between the notes.

Once I noticed we were close to our location our opened my purse and pulled out my black leather gloves.

Lexington's face remained as a plank of wood, his amazement hidden by a slow breath.

"What? You plan on killing someone?"

I ignored him momentarily as I steepled my fingers together to secure my gloves.

"These are all-purpose gloves for your information. They add a touch of class and I could kill in them if necessary. You never know what may jump-off," I gave a one-shoulder shrug as I made sure my twenty-two was loaded with the safety off. "I have a pair your size just in case you needed them."

"I had a surgery years ago that removed one millimeter of skin so the ridges couldn't grow back. I had plastic surgery to repair the aesthetics," he turned his hand palm up.

I gently caressed my hand against his. It was smooth, like silk.

"Isn't this illegal?"

"No. It would be if I were under investigation for a crime."

"Weird."

"You are more prepared than I thought you would be," he jerked his head back.

"I'm not just another pretty face. You'd be surprised by the things that I've done. I'm not new to this. I'm true to this."

"I see. Okay, lil' gansta," he laughed, getting out of the car.

I slid over to follow, "No, wait here."

I followed his line of sight. I saw two black SUVs that seemed like they appeared out of nowhere.

"They've been behind us the entire time?"

"Um, yeah. We'll work on you being aware of your surroundings at all times later. Not new to this, huh?"

He closed the door to the car. Twelve men in black suits entered the restaurant first, with Lexington following closely behind.

I watched him with folded arms and raised eyebrows until he disappeared inside. His thoroughness was turning me on.

Ain't nothing like a man that can handle himself and protect you at the same time.

When Lexington returned, six men were in front of him, with the other six following close on his heels.

He opened the door to the car and extended his hand.

I shifted my weight slightly on him to get my balance as I stepped out in the high heels.

"I got you," Lexington said. His voice was sweet and smooth like syrup as he ran his hand across my butt, smoothing out my skirt.

"Um, thanks," my voice wavered under the weight of his touch.

I was flustered but was determined to hold my composure.

Giovanni was already seated at the table. We were surrounded by jars filled with decorative oils, dried pasta, and hot peppers.

His oversized German Shepherd walked around the restaurant like he was part owner. If patrons would complain, they would just refund them their money and put them out.

The cooks could be heard faintly in the background preparing food. The smell of garlic and oregano was the only welcoming scent in the atmosphere. The tension was thick between all parties present.

Giovanni had a few henchmen near him. You could tell they were packing. I tightened the grip on my purse just in case this went left.

I lowered my head, signaling for Giovanni to speak first.

"Neri doesn't even respect me enough speak to me face to face? I've been in this community back when your grandfather first took over. Things have changed drastically since his death. Your father is...different," he carefully spaced his words.

"Well, that's why-"

"After much consideration, I've dec-," Matteo rudely interrupted me.

"I believe my fiancé was speaking. Giovanni, you don't know me, but I'm sure you know of me. My reputation speaks for itself. Don't disrespect my fiance or me. We're here as a courtesy. What my wife says goes."

A smile parted my lips. The more Lexington revealed himself, the more I fell for him.

To see him so protective of me was starting to erase the reservations I had from our past interaction.

"Giovanni, my father will be retiring soon. When that happens, my fiancé and I will be taking over. It's at my father's request that you remain untouched. As my Lexington mentioned, his reputation speaks for itself. He will not hesitate to kill you. He doesn't care what message it sends to the community. If we must spill blood to get our point across, then we will do just that."

Giovanni's laughter dumped hot coals in the pit of my stomach as he slid back from the table. His eyes squeezed into thin slits.

Slowly, he rose to his feet and proceeded to walk towards the kitchen with his hands clasped behind his back.

I didn't see Lexington's arm coming towards me, pushing me to the floor. At first, I was pissed until I hear gunshots ringing out.

Pop!

Pop!

Pop!

Pop!

A cloud quickly formed from all the gun powder. Lexington and his guys returned fire. I pulled my piece from my purse and emptied my clip.

One of Lexington's men yanked me from the floor and used his body to shield me. Two more ran interference for Lexington so he could follow hot on my trail.

They secured us in our vehicles. Amos knew what was up. He got us out of that tight spot with the quickness.

He cut across three lanes of traffic, careening over the median to speed back in the other direction towards the mansion.

"Let me check you! Are you hit?"

Lexington frantically searched my body for any gunshot or flesh wounds.

"Are you okay?" I yelled, doing the same.

I pulled him into me, nestling my face in his neck, "Thank you for having my back, babe," my eyes rolled skyward.

He forced his spine upright, "Thank you for having my back! We made a good team in there. Not too bad for our first day at work together, huh?"

"Uh-Oh," Lexington sighed when he noticed my father standing outside already waiting on us.

Before the car could come to a complete stop, my dad pulled the door open, "Come here! Are you okay?"

My father did the same thing Lexington did. He checked me over to make sure I wasn't hurt.

"You know how Giovanni is. I kind of expected this from him," I told my dad.

"We didn't kill him only because you asked us not to. Personally, I would order a blackout on his family, but it's up to you how you desire to proceed."

"Giovanni is old blood in the community. His connections and loyalty run deep. I agree though, we must send a message, or everyone will think they can run over us. I can't have you two walking into that. Let me think this out. I don't want it to be a knee-jerk decision. You two get inside and get cleaned up."

"I agree," Lexington said, grabbing me by the waist to escort her inside.

"Lexington?" Neri stopped him.

"Yes?"

"I'm proud of you. My daughter and empire are in good hands. You handled yourself well today, son."

"Thank you."

His words of affirmation made Lexington's spirit soar. He instantly lit up.

I haven't been around his dad much, but he seems to be mean towards Lexington. I was grateful I didn't have to be around him much.

Shootouts were nothing new for me, but it was the other thing that had my guts bubbling with despair.

"What's wrong," Lexington startled me from behind.

"Nothing. I'm okay," I forced a smile.

"No, you're not. We promised to be honest with each other, remember?"

"I remember," I said, sauntering inside of my bedroom. "It doesn't get easier," I confessed.

"What doesn't? The shootouts?

"The killing."

"I don't think any of the shots let out were fatal."

"I could smell the blood. The last time I smelled that much blood, someone was dead," bitterness filled my mouth as I spoke.

He absent-mindedly cracked his knuckles, carefully pondering what he would say.

"It's been hard living through this without anyone to talk to it about," I continued. "I couldn't discuss family business with Grecia. We had a don't ask, don't tell unspoken rule in the house."

"Same here. Taking a life is not to be carried light-heartedly. That's why I pray so much. I hope God understands the position I've been put in since birth. Family is just as important to God as it is to us. I'm not justifying what we do in the name of loyalty, but it is what it is. Prayer does help me, though. Do you want to pray with me?"

"Nah, I'm good. I just want to be alone for right now. I'll be okay. I just need to settle myself and my thoughts."

"Okay, well, I'll let you get cleaned up. I'll be back once I'm done showering. Is that okay?"

"I would like that a lot," I smiled.

Lexington was everything I thought he was back in the day. It's only been a few weeks, but things have been moving so fast.

He's been more like an old friend than a forced lover.

The blood on my clothes made them drop to the floor with a burden I couldn't shake. Despite what Lexington said, I know someone died today.

I'm sure we would find out soon enough who it was.

As the warm water washed over my body, flashes of Lexington springing into action ran through my mind.

There was no hesitation in protecting me. I briefly caught a glimpse of the focus and intensity on his face as he blasted our way out of the restaurant.

It made me think of the safety I felt once by Grecia's side. There was still a gnawing emptiness in my soul where my love for him resided.

I wonder if I will always miss this man? Lexington turned out to be more than I ever imagined but will this fast burn slowly fizzle out over time?

I dried myself off and pulled Lexington's oversized t-shirt over my head. We've been leaving clothes in both rooms because we alternate back and forth with our sleeping arrangements still.

I didn't bother putting on any panties. Lexington has been a perfect gentleman. I wasn't worried about him crossing any lines.

He hasn't put any pressure on me sexually. For that, I was thankful. The attraction is there, but we're both getting out of complicated relationships.

It's been a relief to take our time and find out if we can make our marriage work on an authentic level.

It would be utter agony to be in a forced marriage until the day we die.

Trying to get something outside of each other on the side can be deadly for both of us.

It was just all too much.

The T.V. was watching me once Lexington finally stuck his head in the door. Hours had passed. I know he wanted to give time as I requested.

I was ready to cuddle and go to bed.

"Juanita said this would cheer you up," he used the tray in his hand to push the door open wider.

It was filled with all of my favorites, such as chocolate strawberries, plain Lay's potato chips, pickles, rocky road ice cream, and sparkling apple cider.

"Yessss," I clapped.

"Vikings?"

"You know it," I extended my arms to take the tray from him.

We shared snacks until the tray was nearly empty. Lexington got up and put it on the table.

When he was back in the bed, I curled up in his arms. All I felt was peace as his heartbeat rocked me to sleep.

CHAPTER SEVEN

LEXINGTON CHARLES

I slept so good with Averly in my arms that I didn't hear my alarm. When I woke up, Averly wasn't next to me.

"I thought I heard you stirring around. I would like to invite you out for a breakfast date," she slid her fingers down my chest, leaving their warmth on my skin.

She was coming out of her shell, and it was starting to reveal a softer side to her.

"I will be honored to accompany you on a date."

"Thank you kindly, sir. I want to hear your thoughts about marriage. It will let me know if I need to show up dressed in jeans and a wife-beater or Vera Wang," she chuckled, hopping out of bed.

"Well, let me do my morning devotion and prayer time. I'll meet you downstairs. I can meet you somewhere if you don't want to wait around."

"No, I can wait for you. After yesterday, I would feel safer by your side," her face creased in concern.

"I agree. I'll be ready in an hour."

I grabbed my phone off of the dresser before heading to my room. I had a missed call from my dad. I know he wanted to know what happened regarding the shootout.

I hated talking to him because he was so negative and filled with demands. I already walked away from my life for my family. What else did you want? My blood.

"Are you okay," Averly asked as I walked by her.

"Yeah, my dad called, that's all."

"Your entire countenance changed when you looked at your phone," she spoke in a consoling voice.

"Since I could remember, my father demands excellence. He means well, I guess, it just seems like my best isn't enough most of the time."

"He seemed proud of you the night they announced our union."

"That was all cap. He just wanted to look like a good father in front of you all. It wasn't authentic. Not once has he told me that he was proud of me or that he loved me."

"Not even as a child?"

"Not that I can remember."

"Bummer. Well, my dad is no prize himself, but at least we have each other. I'm glad we're starting to repair our friendship. You didn't know it back then but having you to confide in was an escape for me. You've witnessed firsthand how crazy this all can be."

"I'm glad too. Let me go get dressed and send some prayers up," I pulled Averly into a warm embrace.

I loved that she lingered, and her body no longer tensed up when I touched her.

Once I was inside my room, I went into the walk-in closet to call my dad while I found something to wear.

"Didn't I tell you to check in with me every day?" My father yelled savagely through the phone.

"Do you want me to make this work, or do you want me on the phone with you every day yapping about nothing?"

"Negro watch your tone. What was that shootout about yesterday? I shouldn't have to hear second-hand information. This is now one empire!"

"It won't be one empire officially until we get married. That's why Neri didn't say anything. I just didn't get a chance to call you because I was making sure Averly was good. For some reason, she thinks she dropped a body."

"She did."

"What? Her dad didn't mention anything."

"It didn't get in the wind until late last night. They kept it real hush, hush. Giovanni's nephew he was grooming as his second in command is dead."

"Oh, wow. Any talk about retaliation?"

"That's what you on the inside for! You should know more about this than me. You need to find out what's what! Did you win that girl over yet?"

"So far, so good. She invited me to breakfast to talk about the wedding."

"Good. Get Averly wrapped around your finger so all will work out according to my plan."

"I understand."

"Do you? You know you can be a sucker for love."

"Love is how people manipulate you. I'll never truly love a soul who doesn't have my blood running through their veins."

"Well said, son. I have to go. Find out what's going on with Giovanni and let me know wassup. After this merger, I don't want to be blindsided by an internal war."

"I'm on it."

"Bet," my dad said before hanging up in my face.

Once I was dressed, I dash downstairs. Averly was sitting at the table, murmuring to her dad. She brushed a teardrop from her cheek.

"What's wrong, Averly?"

"Nothing, I'm okay."

"Giovanni's nephew is dead," a slow grin quirked Neri's mouth.

"It's not funny, daddy. This could start a war!"

"It won't. Everyone knows he opened fire on you first. I'm keeping the community from wiping the entire family out. They feel like he stuck first. Lexington has a reputation on the streets as being firm but fair. He's liked, feared, and respected even by his enemies. When they found out he was there, it added insult to injury. They know he would never provoke a war or put you in jeopardy, Averly. Word has spread that you two are a real thing. Besides, Dasante wants to get his work from him. Your father moves a lot of weight even without us in this city. With the better quality heroine, he's going to be able to make a killing."

"You know how I feel about killing dad," Averly sighed.

"You know that I require whatever is necessary to protect our legacy. If blood must be shed, then so be it," he said, cupping her face with both hands.

Averly jerked her head back and stood from the table, "I'm ready to go, Lexington."

She hurried past me.

"Neri, will you be able to talk about this further with me later? I don't know Giovanni like that. I want to know more about his family and their history."

"Absolutely, son," he smiled. "Lexington," he called after me.

"Yes, sir?"

"This is not fake. I've always wanted a son. I know I will never be your father, but I am excited about becoming a father-in-law," he flashed a genuine smile.

"Thank you, Mr. Saccone. I'm looking forward to getting to know you as well."

I don't know if I meant it or not. I'm not sure what type of man Neri is, but I won't completely dismiss him yet.

At this point, anyone would be better than the father I have.

Averly wanted to hunker down at Denny's to discuss our marriage ambitions and plans. I was surprised she didn't want one of those fancy locations to eat.

"I'll have the scrambled eggs with cheese, hash browns, the banana cream pancakes, and white toast. And coffee. Don't' forget the coffee. I like it black," she chopped up her words as if the thoughts were getting stuck in her brain."

"I'll have the same but add turkey bacon."

"Can you add that to mine as well? Thank you."

The waitress nodded and disappeared into the kitchen with our order.

"So, what are your thoughts about marriage?"

Averly dived right in. She didn't wait to try and break the ice or anything.

"I want to know how you are feeling about what went down yesterday?"

"I told you I was fine. Let's move on," her face was hard as she spoke.

"Okay. I won't push, but if you need me. I'm here. My beliefs about what marriage is are quite simple. You're partners. As your partner, I'll extend the grace you need daily to grow into your best self. I pledge my loyalty and pure love until the day I die, and then even after that. I want to inhale your exhales just to be filled with all of you. Your spouse is your best friend. No secrets or judgments belong in our space. You are free to be you so that there can be a we. Finally, marriage is forever for me. Not because of the community or the contract, but because I'm only doing this once. I don't believe in divorce, but I will fund a funeral."

"Well, then," she pressed her hand to her mouth to stifle a giggle.

I hoped she knew I was serious. Forced or not, we were in this for the long haul.

"I don't want to make you feel any type of way. Have you and your father's relationship always been this way? Things changed with my dad and me after my mother died."

She waited until she swallowed her food before exhaling, "Yeah, pretty much. When my mother was alive, she just brought balance. She was the loving and encouraging one. Since you all in my Kool-Aid."

"What about your mother's side? Do you ever talk to them?"

"Geez, Louise! Would you like my bra and panty size too?"

"Soon, but not yet."

She looked down to avoid making eye contact. She was cute when she was embarrassed. Her stubbornness constantly made her force her emotions back down.

"No, when my mother married my dad, they cut her off. To them, she was already dead long before the car accident. Growing up, we never went around them. To this day, I've never met that side of my family. You could be my cousin for all I know," she erupted into laughter, breaking the depression that started to sit on us.

"Definitely not your cousin," I joined her.

"You know you don't have to do what you did yesterday. I can handle that from here on out, Averly. Taking lives will be my burden to bear, not yours."

She straightened her shoulders as a mask of reserve covered her face.

"No, I don't like it, but I do what I must to keep my family safe. That's something you need to know about me. I may be a brat, but family is everything to me. There's no length I wouldn't go to to keep you safe or protect you."

"I thought you hated my guts."

"You're wearing me down," she chuckled. "How do you feel about kids?"

"I know we have a crazy life, but I still want children. If and when you do get pregnant, you need to make it special for me. Take me out to a romantic dinner, buy me some flowers or something, make me feel like you are trying to get it for the first time," he smiled from ear to ear.

"Boy, stop it!"

"I'm for real. That's special for me. To become a father is one of the highest honors I could achieve next to being your husband."

She shifted uncomfortably in her seat.

"If you'll have me," I continued.

"Yes, I will," she leaned over the table, meshing her lips with mine.

Averly and I were experiencing a different type of connection and intimacy. We both loved the people we were with, but they could never understand the burdens we carried in the name of family. They would never understand the blood we shed and be able to sleep next to us at night without fear tormenting them.

We could be ourselves with one another.

"How do you feel about moving out once we're married?"

"Absolutely! I hate living back at home in my old bedroom!"

"I want to show you this place I've picked out for us. I hope you like it."

"You seem to have good taste. You have a fifty-fifty chance of nailing this."

"I see. Do you have plans for us tomorrow?" I asked her.

"No, why?"

"I want to meet up with the guys to fill them in about the wedding."

"You mean to tell them how I've been driving you crazy?" She sucked her teeth.

"What? Would I do a thing like that?"

"I don't know you like that. Maybe you would."

"You wrong."

"Uh-hum," she stuffed a forkful of pancakes in her mouth.

We spent the rest of breakfast talking about nothing in particular. It was like we were back in high school again. Just choppin' it up.

We told each other almost everything. I'm grateful to have another chance with Averly. I forgot how peaceful it is in her presence.

I've always struggled with keeping anything for myself. I felt it was selfish to do so, but Averly may be the exception.

*   *   *

Last night we slept in my room. I still felt out of sorts in the mansion, but it wasn't as bad as when I first got here.

Neri has his ways, but it was nice to have him encourage and support my business decisions.

Things were going well with Averly. I've told her more about myself than I have ever been able to tell Chastity.

I could be myself with Avery. My dark side and the things that I had to do for the business and family didn't scare her.

"Aht. Aht. Where are you going dressed like a whore?"

"What are you talking about?"

"That grey sweatsuit you have on. You know the kind of attention that draws. You want to be a slut so bad!"

"A slut?"

"Yeah, play stupid if you want to. Let me know when you are really dressed."

"You're kidding, right?" I laughed.

"Nah, my mans. You need to find something more appropriate. Do you want me out here in this see-through thot wear gracing the fashion world right now?"

"Enough said. Dang Averly. We just chilling. We ain't even about to do nothing but hang out at the pool hall."

"Good, hang out in some jeans and a nice t-shirt if you still want to be casual," she smirked.

"You know what? I don't want any smoke, woman. I want this same energy when I ask you to change out of something inappropriate."

"I got you."

I was shocked that Averly tripped about me wearing my sweatpants out of the house.

Was she jealous?

I know I felt some type of way when I saw her with Grecia. I was confused at how I reacted to her being with him behind my back.

I guess we are feeling each other more than we want to admit.

I went into my closet and pulled out a pressed designer button-up and a pair of Dolce & Gabbana bleached print jeans.

I splashed on some Creed Aventus as I looked myself over once more.

Yeah, if I were her, I would be tripping too. A nigga fine in real life.

"Is this better," I asked Averly on my way out.

"Um...yeah, I guess," desire flashed in her eyes.

Let me find out she *really* wants me.

"You guess, huh?"

"Boy, you know you look like you have been dipped in butter. Gone on and leave me alone. Drop your location so we can meet up to go pick out a cake and invitations for this wedding."

"Do we have enough time to get all that together?"

"We're rich, Lexington. We can move mountains, feel me?"

"Yeah, I feel you. I'll drop my location. You can stop by whenever. I want you to meet my peoples anyway. We've been together since we were shorties."

"Aww."

"Cut it out," I waved her off as I headed out.

"I can't get a kiss?"

"You want a kiss?"

"Yeah, I do," she sauntered over into my personal space.

I slid my arm around her waist and placed my other hand behind her neck as our tongues passionately entwined.

"Make sure you come by, Averly. I want to show off my fiancé."

"I am. Promise."

When I walked into the pool hall, I scanned the room with my eyes looking for my guys.

"Bout time you make it here!" Freddie yelled.

"Man, chill out."

We all shook up. Freddie and Reno were my brothers from another mother. I kept my circle small and tight.

Freddie was the jokester, loud and outgoing, but he wouldn't hesitate to blow someone down to keep me safe. Reno is laid back and quiet. He was the deadliest of us all.

The nigga lowkey a serial killer. Everybody that he dropped was planned with precision. We were skilled in torture and could track anyone down.

There's nowhere you could hide to get away from him. He was a genius. Not just hood smart either. He was MIT smart. He graduated from there to prove a point to a teacher who told him he would never amount to anything but a gang banger.

"So, how is engagement life going?"

"Man, to be honest, it was rough at first, but it's starting to smooth out."

"I thought this was some elaborate plan to infiltrate their organization until I saw you both interacting at the engagement party," Freddie said.

"Do we have a plan?" Reno's eyebrows were wrinkled together.

"There is no plan. You know me and Averly had a thing back in the day."

"That girl hated you after you stood her up in high school," Freddie erupted in laughter.

"Look, we got past all of that. Now she's my Apple Cinnamon."

"Apple Cinnamon? Nigga what is this? The next installment of Love Jones?" Freddie was not letting up.

"Well, I happy for you, but I don't trust none of them. I'm ready for whatever, whenever. Feel me?" Reno stressed.

"I wouldn't expect anything less," I nodded at him.

"What is it like over there with the opps?"

"It was tense at first. Of course, you know I stay on my toes. It's cool, I guess."

"Bro, why y'all rushing to get married? That's making all of this look real suspect. Y'all both were public with other people now y'all getting married?" Freddie pried.

"I can't explain it. That love we had from that past ignited when we linked back up. If it weren't for my mama dying, y'all know I would've still been with Averly."

"Nigga, y'all wasn't even dating. She wanted you to be her first. You act like y'all were high school sweethearts or something," Freddie kept rambling out what I'm sure everyone has been thinking.

Reno just concentrated on lining the white ball up with his next target on the green turf.

"We were something better. Best friends. We got to know everything about each other with no judgments or ulterior motives. Neither one of us could tell the people we were in relationships with about what went down in the communities we operated in. It's just a different vibe with Averly. We picked up where we left off, and I'm feeling it."

"Well, if you like it, we love it," Reno finally spoke up.

We spent the next couple of hours catching up. Reno beat us round after round on the pool table.

It was still early in the day, so we opted for beer instead of hard liquor.

"There goes Wifey," Reno mumbled.

"Yeah, I want her to meet y'all."

"Hey, babe. Am I too early?"

Averly had on these white jeans that were so tight they looked like an extension of her flesh. Her red off-shoulder sweater accented her collar bone. She wore her hair wild, but it was sexy the way it rested on her shoulders.

"No, you're good. This is Reno," he extended his hand to her. "And this is Freddie."

He lifted her hand to his mouth and kissed her hand.

"Nigga, you done lost your mind. I will chop your hand off and send yo' mama a finger every year on the anniversary of your death if you don't stop playing on my top about my woman!"

"Babe, it's okay."

"Wait for me by the bar, baby," I demanded.

Averly looked uncomfortable, but she did what I asked.

We all waited for her to walk away, "Freddie, don't play with me like that. You know I don't play about my women."

"Lex, chill out, man. You know I didn't mean anything by that. You really are feeling her, huh?"

"You thought I was lying? I'm rearranging my entire life for her. I love her, man!"

They stood there in shock. I was with Chastity for years and never professed my love for her to them.

"My bad, man. It won't happen again."

"If y'all bringing a plus one, make sure to let me know," I advised them.

"Alright," they replied in unison as I laid my stick on the table.

I tossed my empty bottle in the trash as I headed towards Averly.

Her face was twisted in concern, "What was that about?"

"I have a jealous streak. Now you know."

"I don't want to cause problems with you and your friends."

"No, if I don't like something, I'm going to check it on sight. No exceptions. I don't believe in letting things build up to a point where I explode. That happened once, and I vowed it would never happen again. I also wanted to make it clear in the door that you are mine. People aren't going to think things are sweet, and they can handle you just because we moved fast."

Averly just stood there with a crooked smile of admiration on her face.

"So, what's first?" I asked her.

"I need to get a headcount as soon as possible."

"For someone who doesn't want to get married, you're making a lot of plans."

"You better be glad you just have to show up. I've wanted to get married since I was five. The circumstances aren't traditional, but I want my wedding to be. Getting to know you is making me feel like I can have the wedding of my dreams somewhat."

"I'm glad you feeling me."

"Just a little."

"So much cap," I laughed. "How would you feel about going to church with me tomorrow?"

"I'm not against it. I'll go with you."

CHAPTER EIGHT

AVERLY GRACE

I took three deep breaths as I walked up the concrete pathway into the church. It was a small but modern building. You could tell it was new construction. Thick doors separated the sanctuary from the entry area.

The greeters smiled at us both while an usher handed us a program. We were ushered to our seats near the front. The pew creaked when we sat down. They must've had some water damage at some point because the carpet smelled musty. It could be the lady in front of me, who knows?

The pastor's message was very encouraging. He said that despite not having all the details of a plan, it was important to keep moving forward. I cast my gaze on the gold cross that hung behind the preacher. I wondered how Lexington put so much faith in someone he has never seen? It couldn't be me.

"The map to the finish line may not look the way we desire it to, but as long as we finish, that's all that matters," the preacher belted as the parishioners showered him with Hallelujahs.

I looked over to Lexington, who was hanging on his every word. He was highlighting in his bible and writing notes on his program from the sermon.

I thought we would be leaving immediately after church, but we lingered until the pastor's assistant walked over to us.

"Mr. Charles, the pastor is ready to see you both now."

"Thank you."

Once she was several steps in front of us, I leaned in to whisper in his ear, "What is happening?"

"You know it's important for me to get married in a church. I take my vows seriously. I'm going to make them before my pastor."

"I'm good with that, but we just couldn't book the church?"

"No, he wants to talk to us. If he's going to marry us, he wants to know a bit about us."

I was surprised this man went this far. It made me feel good that he was starting to be just as invested in our union as I was.

"Please, come in and have a seat," the pastor motioned for us to sit in two purple chairs in front of him. "So, you're getting married? From what Lexington told me, things are moving rather quickly."

"Yes, an old flame we had from high school has us both smitten with each other all over again," Lexington was lying in this preacher's face.

"Young love is so grand. Have you had marriage counseling?" The pastor asked.

"I don't know him well enough to need counseling," I chuckled.

The pastor didn't find it amusing. His expression wasn't judgmental, but it was more one of concern.

"I would love for us to have counseling pastor."

I was shocked, but Lexington has been so sweet about everything that I couldn't deny him this. If this is important to him, it's important to me.

"I would as well. Every bit helps. I do know marriage requires both of us to work on it daily."

"Yes, it does," the pastor smiled at me.

The pastor handed us a schedule of sessions. Despite us getting married soon, he still wanted us to continue all the sessions even after getting married.

That was not a bad idea. Right now, we're cool because we just linked back up, but who's to say in a few months we're not trying to kill each other.

Marriage counseling reinforced the peace I was starting to have about marrying Lexington Charles.

"Um, we have an engagement party tomorrow," I blurted as we approached our car in the parking lot.

"What? Averly we just had a party. Besides, who plans a party on a Monday?"

"I do, and that wasn't a party. That was a meet and greet with the community's leaders to solidify our merger."

"It's last minute. No one will show, and it will be a waste of money."

"It's going to be something small and intimate. You know how important it is for me to have my total wedding experience. This party is a big deal for me. Can you get Reno and Freddie to come?"

"That won't be a problem."

"They can bring someone if they'd like."

"I will let them know, babe."

"Babe, huh?"

"Shut up, jerk," he shoved me gently.

I was enjoying getting reacquainted with all sides of Lexington.

"After we get done, you want to finish watching Vikings?"

"You know it. I told you that you would like it."

"Yeah, once I got used to all of the gore."

"Girl, we were just in a shoot-out the other day. You know you've seen worse."

"I know, but they have it in slow motion. It's something about when they use swords."

"I feel you."

"Before we do that, I want to make you dinner."

"Girl, can you even cook?"

"You're a hater," I giggled, watching him make a beeline for my door.

"Stop playing with me. I told you not to touch a car door in my presence."

"My bad. I need to stop by the store on the way home to pick up what I want to cook for dinner."

"Okay."

Lexington and I drove to church together, but our security detail was still following us. A few were inside of the church while the others waited outside like they were Secret Service Agents.

"Can you let them know we don't need all of them to go inside Lexington?"

"I got you."

He got out of the car and spoke with the security team. When he was done, he opened my car door to let me out.

I watched him wipe the basket down before he grabbed hold of it.

"You want me to push the basket?"

"Nah, I'm good," he said.

Two guards followed behind us. Far enough not to gain attention but close enough to spring into action if need be.

"I'm making Salmon with Brussel sprouts."

"Jumping out into the deep, ain't you?"

"I'm going to show you, watch."

My chest stuttered when I noticed Grecia coming towards us.

Lexington must've too because he pushed me behind him.

"Look, don't come over here with no beef, man."

Grecia waved off his words like mosquitoes.

"I'm not about to get permission to interact with a woman whose tongue been over every inch of my body."

Our security team was now standing between Grecia and us.

"Nigga that disrespect gone get you killed out here. Watch ya' mouth before I run in it."

"Nigga, you think you tough with that security team around you twenty-four-seven, but you can still get touched."

"Nigga, I don't need this security team. You keep trying me you gone need to hire one for your granny. I move differently. I'll end the existence of your entire bloodline without hesitation. Find you somebody else to play with because this ain't it."

"Averly, you can't speak for yourself now? You had plenty to say at the gun range."

"You're out of order, Grecia. That was then, and this is now. I'm with Lexington. What we had is dead. You had a chance to make me your wife, and you didn't. Some men know what they want and do what it takes to solidify it. Now you have to watch another man love me."

"Yeah? We'll see about that," he grinned like an ancient serpent, tricking foolish Eve all over again.

We all watched him walk away. I knew that he was up to something in my gut, but I'm not sure what it is.

"Are you okay?" I asked Lexington.

"Yeah, I'm good. Your ex be popping up everywhere. At this point, he like a herpes outbreak."

"I know. I didn't see Grecia this much when we were together. That nigga loved the streets more than he loved me."

"And you were still going to marry him?"

"Yeah, I thought that was love at the time."

"And now?"

"Now, I'm learning about a different type of love. A love that is patient and kind."

"You've been reading my bible, huh?"

"Yeah, first Corinthians thirteen and one. Love is patient, love is kind. It does not envy, it does not boast, it is not proud. It is not rude, it its not self-seeking, it is not easily angered, it keeps no records of wrongs. Love does not delight in evil but rejoices with the truth. We may have been forced into this, but things have changed. Your love has exemplified this. Your love is making me a better woman."

Lexington just smiled while entwining his fingers with mine. I wasn't all on board with his God, but I did like reading the bible.

We got the rest of what I needed to make his salmon and left the store.

I didn't see any sign of Grecia when we left. Other than the random text here and there, I haven't heard from him.

Knowing him, he was planning something, but I'm not sure how far he's going to take it.

Sometimes I wish he would move on. Other times, I want him to wait just in case what I'm feeling with Lexington turns out to be a facade that he's putting on.

I would be devastated if this were all a ruse from Lexington.

It was easy for me to fall for him all over again once I found out why he left me hanging. I've been fighting my infatuation with him. I daydream about how his body would feel on top of mine. Passion took hold of me every time I allowed my mind to wonder.

"Are you sure you're okay?" Lexington asked again as we pulled off.

"Yeah, Grecia has always been a bit disrespectful at times. It's nothing new."

"Did you ever put his hands on you, Averly Grace?"

His words hummed inside of my head like a nest of angry hornets some fool poked with a stick.

"Um..."

"That nigga was hitting you, Averly?" He shot me a furious glance.

"Not all the time," I drew a shallow breath.

"I'm going to kill him!" He smashed the brake to the floor.

"Lexington, please just leave it alone. We're together now. That's my past."

"If he even blinks at you hard, I'm killing that nigga on God!"

His aggression was turning me on. I was curious if he brought this same energy into the bedroom. I had to find out before we got married. I mean, you can't be married, and the sex is wack.

After the engagement party, that's when I'll put it on him.

*   *   *

"You look amazing," Lexington uttered slowly when I appeared before him in the hallway in my black dress.

I could hear the murmurs of servers and staff, making sure everything is on point as I requested.

My dress was to die for. It was black with gold embellishments. The side split went up to my hip and was embellished with gold trim and rhinestones.

Lexington wore a black three-piece suit that was tailored to perfection, as usual.

"Thank you," I smiled, hooking my arm around his.

We only invited a handful of people we knew would celebrate what appeared to be an irrational decision.

I stepped through the expansive doorway with double doors that led out to the rooftop. I needed some fresh air.

"What's wrong?" Lexington asked, sliding up behind me, wrapping both arms around my waist.

"This was nice. I'm glad everyone we invited made it."

"Me too. Whatever makes you smile, I'm down for it."

He planted slow, soft kisses on the back of my neck.

"I want to make love to you tonight."

"Are you sure you're ready for that?"

"I mean, we both need to test the waters. It doesn't mean anything. We're both human. I can't speak for you, but I ain't had none since we linked up."

"Same here. So, you just need to get your rocks off, is what you're saying?"

"Exactly that. We're attracted to one another, and we're about to get married. We might as well give it a go."

"Girl, you need to romance me and stop treating me like I'm some easy piece of meat. Put some respect on my man's woman."

"Whatever."

It seemed like it took an eternity for all of our guests to leave.

When everyone had cleared out, Lexington and I went upstairs.

"Grab an overnight bag."

"What? What's going on?" I asked him."

"I got a surprise for you," he bit down on his lower lip, trying not to laugh.

"What are you up to?"

"You have ten minutes."

"I don't have time to change?"

"Nope. You're wasting your ten minutes."

I kicked my heels off in the hallway and bolted into my bedroom to toss some things into my spennanight bag.

I didn't bother changing because I wasted some of my time asking questions. I didn't want Lexington to leave me.

I was playing hard, but I was feeling this man. I just wanted to make sure I made him earn me even though my dad gave me over to him freely.

"I'll carry it," Lexington reached for my bag.

He was waiting for me still in the hallway.

"Where are we going?"

The staff had pulled our Maybach around to the front. Lexington helped me inside of the car.

"Here, put this on. I'm not asking you; I'm telling you. I'm also not about to argue with you about it or answer a million questions. Just put it on Averly."

I slowly exhaled the breath that was caught in my throat. Lexington was aggressive but in a good way. He had balance. He was so caring and considerate that I knew it was because it involved my best interest when he was aggressive.

I did as he asked and put on the blindfold.

"You better not be trying to kill me."

"Girl, hush."

Summer Walker's words danced in the atmosphere in the car. Her newest release, '*Over It*,' was an entire vibe.

Lexington gently placed his hand on my shaking leg, "Relax. You're in good hands."

After about twenty minutes, the car came to a stop.

"Not yet!" Lexington yelled when I reached for my blindfold. "You are just hard-headed."

I heard someone open my door and grab my hand.

"I got her," Lexington told them. "Okay, you have a step. I'll tell you when. Okay, step."

"I feel like I'm going to trip and fall."

"Well, you better learn quickly to follow my instructions and trust me."

We walked several feet and I heard the elevator ring.

"Step," Lexington instructed me further.

I could feel us going upward. I gathered that we were most likely in a hotel.

"Okay, step," he continued.

He kept a firm grip on my arm until we came to a stop. I heard the door click, and we stepped inside.

"Okay, take it off."

Tears immediately filled my eyes, "What is this?"

"I have to redo the night I broke your heart. It's why you hated me all this time."

"But you told me why. I forgave you for that night."

"Yeah, but I still want my chance to make it special."

I took in the view of the room. He had bleeding-heart flowers all over the room. He remembered these are my favorite flower.

I was speechless as I took it all in. Every fiver in my body was taunt with adoration. Lexington was winning me over with every gesture.

"When did you have time to do all of this? You paid someone?"

"No, when I was out running errands before the dinner. I set it all up then. My father owns it, so it wasn't hard. Now finding them flowers was another story."

I could feel a swirl of nervous knots in my stomach, "Can you unzip me?"

I seductively turned so that he could see the gold zipper standing between him and my nakedness. He skimmed his lips along the sweep of my cheek.

After spinning me around, he cradled my face in his hands as he kissed me passionately. It was deep and in a way he never has before.

Without missing a beat, he reached down and released me from my dress.

My heart dropped to the ground with it. He picked me up and carried me to the bed.

He laid me down gently.

"What?" I asked him as he stood over me.

His eyes blazed with longing, "I've waited years for this moment to show you how much I'm feeling you physically."

As he towered over me, I just knew tonight would be everything I needed it to be.

*   *   *

The next morning I woke up in Lexington's arms.

"Good morning, beautiful," Lexington placed sensual kisses on my neck and cheek.

"Morning."

"They'll be bringing breakfast up soon. Would you like to see the house I picked out for us before we go back to the mansion?"

"I would love to. You may have us held up in some shack or something."

There was a tap on the door, "Room service," the lady on the other side yelled.

Lexington gently pulled his arm from under me. I peeked under the comforter at my naked body. I quickly tried to fumble around for my panties but couldn't find them.

Lexington sat the tray down on the bed and bent down, "Here they are," he grinned devilishly.

"Give me those!"

I slid under the covers. I don't know why I was embarrassed, but I was.

I quickly put them on and pulled the covers back over my breast.

"Here, put this on," Lexington handed me his t-shirt.

I inhaled deeply as I pulled it over my head. It still smelled like his cologne from the previous night.

"I know I'm acting weird compared to the porn star I was acting like last night."

"That you were," he bit down on his bottom lip.

"Don't judge me," I tossed the pillow at him.

"I'm trying not to attack you again before we leave. I just didn't want to overstep. I mean, you did say it didn't mean anything. We were kind of making sure we had sexual chemistry."

"I did say that, huh?"

There was this awkward silence between us. Flashes of him pleasing my body in every way imaginable bombarded my mind.

I hated to admit it, but he was so much better than Grecia. He was only the second person I've ever been with, but it was a difference in how he touched me while we were intimate.

You would've thought we'd been together for years the way my body responded to him.

I watched him dip the strawberry in the whipped cream and place it in my mouth.

He took his finger and wiped the excess cream from my lip.

"You should know by now I'm a messy eater."

"So am I," he smirked.

I started to choke as a flashback of his head between my legs hit me.

I gently slapped my hand against my chest, trying to get the strawberry down the right pipe.

"Are you okay?"

I struggled but finally caught my breath. I quickly gained my composure.

"Yea, it just went down the wrong pipe."

"Well, as soon as your ready, we can shower and get dressed."

"Okay."

"So, what do you have on your agenda today?"

"Just trying to get this wedding stuff wrapped up. I don't want it to look like we rushed to get married. I'm trying to fit the wedding of my dreams into a small timeframe. Luckily, I've had ideas buried for years."

"Wow, really?"

"Yes, I saw my mother in her wedding dress and fell in love with having that moment for myself. It wasn't just the dress, though. It was the way she and my dad looked at each other. I wanted to look in my husband's eyes and see forever."

"Wanted?"

"Yeah, I don't know if I'll have that with you. It's like we're getting married, then dating. You could leave dirty boxers all over the house or pick your toes in bed. I don't know. I won't find out until after we've said I do."

"I think we're going to be okay."

"You sound confident."

"Why not? You can be selfish at times, but other than that, you're cool."

"I'm cool, huh?"

"Yeah, the outside aesthetics are pleasing to the eye, but you would've said that was shallow."

"And I've been working on not being selfish."

"Yes, you have. I can't take that from you."

"We let this breakfast get cold. I'm going to jump in the shower so we can get our day started."

"Bet."

I tossed a glance over my shoulder. Lexington's eyes were liquid pools of desire.

I wanted nothing more than to invite him to shower with me to continue what we started last night, but I decided not to get chocolate wasted.

"What?"

"Um...nothing."

"Oh, look like you wanted something."

"Lexington...," his name felt smooth against my tongue, slightly cool. I licked my lips as if savoring its sweetness.

"Yes," the low and pleasant hum from his voice warmed my blood.

"Lord have mercy," I whispered.

"We grown lady," he licked his lips as he read my body.

"Nah, I better not. I don't want sex to confuse this more than what it already is."

"Understood," one heavy eyebrow slanted in strong disapproval.

I quickly disappeared into the bathroom with my overnight bag.

I wasn't in the shower for more than thirty minutes. Suddenly, being trapped in the hotel room with Lexington felt claustrophobic.

When I came out, he was already dressed.

"You didn't want to shower first?"

"I used the room next door. My dad does own the hotel, remember? I ain't no dirty nigga now."

"I wasn't-"

"It's cool. You ready?"

The fire between us was now ice-cold glaciers. The residue of last night quickly wore off.

"Is something wrong?"

"Nah, let's just go," he pulled open the door so that I could walk out first.

Our security team met us downstairs. The valet had pulled around our Maybach.

I reached for Lexington's hand, but he quickly pulled it back and stuffed it in his pocket.

Overcast skies turned everything dreary and cold. It matched the vibe between us. I was just waiting to get out of his presence at this point.

"I didn't mean-"

Pop!

Pop!

Pop!

"Get down!"

Lexington and the security team both yelled, but I already had my gun in my hand, busting back.

It all went down so fast I couldn't see the color of the car or anything.

"Get her home, now!" Lexington yelled.

The security team pushed me in the back seat and sped off.

This was just one more thing for the chief of police to nag to my dad about.

He was still covering up the press from what went down at the restaurant.

My heart felt like it was going to drop out of my booty hole.

I've never been under fire like this. It seems like since we merged our empires with Lexington's family, it's happening more and more. Someone doesn't want this merger to happen.

My dad wasn't there when I made it back to the mansion.

"What's wrong *mi amor*," Juanita grabbed me by my shoulders.

"Someone was shooting at us!"

"Again?"

"I know! Something is off!"

"Where is Lexington?"

"He stayed behind to go after the shooters."

I desperately fumbled through my purse for my phone.

Once the call connected, it just rang until it went to voicemail. I knew better than to call Lexington.

I paced back and forth. With every step, it felt as if my lungs were getting tighter and tighter.

The tires screeched as the truck careened to a stop. Lexington jumped out before it was in park good.

He almost toppled over me getting into the house.

"Did you get hit?"

He frantically checked my body like a madman.

"I'm good, babe! Are you okay?"

"Yeah, I'm good, baby."

"Were y'all able to catch up to them?"

"Nope. I'm firing your father's security team and bring mine in except for Amos. This is unacceptable. Your father already agreed to it. Ain't no way we should keep ending up in shoot-outs with a security team. They rats."

"I agree. Something has been off. I was worried about you! I know I'm sending you mixed signals but today made me realize how much I've gotten used to having you around me. I don't want to lose you before I find out if it's worth it or not.'

"So you want to make sure the best thing that ever happened to you can still happen, huh?" He laughed.

"Basically," I wrapped my arms around him like that hug had always been inside of me, waiting to come out.

I caught a glimpse of my father out of the corner of my eye. He had this goofy grin on his face. He didn't say anything. He just went into his office and closed the door.

"You were acting like you were worried about a real nigga," he kissed me on my forehead.

"Go upstairs and get undressed. I'm about to show you how much," I told him.

"Oh yeah? You just-"

"That was then. The way things have been going lately, I see I can't take any opportunity for happiness for granite. I can't be afraid to live and take chances. I want to see what we can be Lexington. I know it was crazy circumstances but each time, we stand together and get through the moment...as a team. Let me love you down."

"I'm here for all of that, Averly. I'll meet you upstairs."

"Okay, I'm going to grab some snacks because I know we're going to work up an appetite."

"We need to be in a shootout more often. It seems like that's the only way to get your guards down."

"They're not all the way down. I just want to give you a real chance."

"I appreciate that. I'm not trying to play you or play with ya' baby girl. I promise."

"I believe you. Let me check in with my dad, and I'll be right up."

"No rush. I'll be in my room. Your bed too small, babe. We need some space."

"Okay, that's fine."

He gave me another quick peck on the forehead before disappearing upstairs.

My knuckles gently tapped on the door.

"Come in," my daddy called from the other side.

"You heard about what happened?"

"Yeah, Lexington called me on his way home. He said it was someone who used to work for his father, Dasante."

"He just told me he didn't catch up with them."

"He didn't, but his one friend was able to hack the street cameras. I think he said his name is Reno or something. Anyways, he assured Lexington it would be taken care of tonight. I'm sure he doesn't want you to worry. After the restaurant, can you blame him?"

"It seems like since we've merged with them that we've been under fire. First, Giovanni and now someone from their side?"

"Well, the person from their side doesn't work with them anymore. Something about a disgruntled employee."

"He shot at people in broad daylight. I would say he's past disgruntled."

"You have that right. I see things are going well between you and Lexington. I knew you two would be a good match."

"You didn't know, and you don't care, daddy. Just stop the charade."

"I know I don't have that nurturing touch like your mother. A part of me died with her. I'm sorry I haven't been there for you, Averly. You must know that I love you. My ways may not be the best, but sometimes, they do work out. I messed a lot of things up, but I'm trying to make it right. I promise I am."

"Well, tell me where my mother is buried."

He narrowed his eyes, "Get married, produce an heir, and I'll think about it."

"Why is it such a secret?" I yelled.

"Because I don't want the wrong people to find out where she is buried."

"The wrong people? What does that mean?"

"Goodbye, Averly."

I stormed out of his office, more determined than ever to find out the truth behind my mother's death.

I was unphased by his new set of lies. My dad did this once a quarter. He would act like he had remorse for abandoning me when my mother died, but he would do something narcissistic.

Toxicity oozed from my father like liquor from the pores of a drunk. I didn't take anything he said to heart.

At the end of the day, he could care less if Lexington was good for me or not. All he cared about was getting out of debt and getting those commas back in his bank account.

"Hey, Chica," Juanita sang. "What do you need?"

"Just a lil' sexy tray of snacks for Lexington and me."

"Look at you. So things are going well, I presume?"

"Yeah, we decided to give this a real chance. We've been in situations where our lives have been in each other's hands, and we held it down. He told me about what happened that night you had to pick me up in high school," I dropped my tone to speak softly.

I was grown now, but the last thing I needed was to hear about Juanita coming to pick me up from the hotel without telling him.

I don't know what he would do to her! She was the closest thing I had to a mother now. I would always protect her at all costs.

"What happened?"

"His mother died," I slumped.

"Awe. I knew it had to be something like that. I knew his nanny. He was always a good boy. I thought it was out of character for him. I'm glad you worked it out."

"Guess what?"

"What?" She leaned in to sip on this hot tea.

"He surprised me and took me to the same hotel after the engagement party last night."

"What!"

"Yes! He even decorated the room like it was that night in high school."

"That is so romantic. I think he'll be good for you. I really do. The dresses are ready. I'm picking them up tomorrow. I'm thrilled that you made me your maid of honor!"

"Who else is going to stand by my side? You're all I have in this world. I wish mama were still here, and I miss her terribly, but I'm grateful that God left me, you."

"She'll always be with you, *mi amor*," she hugged me.

She quickly put some cheese, meats, grapes, and strawberries on the tray.

"Do you want me to put it in the refrigerator until he gets back?"

"What do you mean, get back?"

"He went out while you were in your dad's office."

"Hum, maybe he got a call from his dad or something. After what happened today, I wouldn't be surprised. Let me get my phone out of my purse. He most likely left me a message."

I went over to the foyer and picked up my purse from the table. I tossed it there when I came in.

I pulled out my phone, and there was nothing from Lexington.

I blew his line down. I called him back to back, and nothing. He started sending me to voicemail.

The next number I dialed was to his personal guard, "Hump, where is he?"

"Ms. Saccone-"

"Don't play with me! Where is he?"

"He's at...Chastity's," he said, barely audible.

Hump was the head of Lexington's security. He was built like Debo but looked like Snoop Dog in the face.

"Text me the address, and I mean right now!"

"Is everything okay?"

"Nah, but I'm about to make it okay," I ran past Juanita to change into my jeans, t-shirt, and my stomp a trick out Jordan's."

I put my holster on under my shirt and made sure my Glock was loaded. Lexington is going to learn quickly that I don't play about my feelings.

I hope his ex shoots back.

CHAPTER NINE

LEXINGTON CHARLES

Hump texted me that Averly was on her way. I wasn't mad at him for telling her. She was about to be my wife. I didn't want them thinking they needed to cover me. I stood ten toes down on any decision I made.

"Averly on her way over here," I tossed a glance at Chastity before looking back down at my phone.

I wasn't sure if Averly would try to text me, but she was blowing my line down for sure.

"What do you mean she's on her way over here?"

"Our security team told her I was here. I didn't get a chance to tell her I was leaving. When you called and told me what happened, I rushed over here."

"I don't want her at my house!"

"You don't have a choice," I gave a one-shoulder shrug.

"I most definitely do!"

"I pay the bills here; that's why you called me about what happened. Soon she's going to be my wife. I'm not trying to piss you off, but that's just what it is."

"So much for me still having you on the side. You sound committed to me," Chastity scoffed.

I looked past her and saw Averly storming up the walkway through the opened blinds. I've never seen her dressed down in jeans and a plain shirt.

Even thugged out, she was sexy.

"You better stand down, Hump," her glare sliced him up like confetti. "I'll tear everything up in this house if your boss thinks he about to play with me!"

She pushed by him and knocked on the door.

Chastity got to it before I could. She was thirsty to let Averly know who she was.

"I'm here to see my fiancé Lexington Charles. Is he here?"

"Where else would he be?"

"Play with it if you want. I do pistol play. I hope he told you that. Don't let this light skin fool you lil' mama."

She rolled her eyes and walked away.

"Calm down, Averly!"

Smack!

"I can't believe I fell for all those lies that fell from your lying lips! I was foolish enough to sleep with you thinking we're giving this a real chance! You're so foul! You had the nerve to drag me out of the gun range with Grecia, but you over here laid up with your ex!"

"I'm not laid up, Chastity. I can explain w-"

"Don't bother! Stay here with this low-budget bottom feeder. I don't need you! Never have! Never will! You the same nigga from high school!"

"Who you calling a bottom feeder?"

She launched herself into a spinning leap toward Averly. She lunged forward to meet her, jabbing her fist towards Chastity's face. She countered with a quick jab to my eye.

"Stop it!" I scolded them both.

Me, Hump, and the rest of the security team struggled to pull them apart. They had a grip on each other's hair.

Averly's Jordan's scuffed and kicked at the cobbles as I dragged and manhandled her all the way to the truck.

"Get her home," I roared at Amos.

"You need to keep your little pet under control before I hurt her!"

"Girl, you lucky she didn't shoot you. Don't talk about her like that!" I told Chastity.

"You have caught feelings for her, haven't you? You are really falling for her!" She screamed.

"Yeah, I am."

"That was fast! I can't believe you! All you niggas the same! I swear!" She slammed the door in my face.

I shook my head and headed to my truck. Hump opened my door so that I could get in.

I had mixed feelings. I hated hurting Chastity, but lately, Averly and I have been in the trenches.

I've never been able to share that side of me with Chasity or that part of my world even.

Averly and I are bonding differently. I'm not going to lie like what we've built in this short period is anywhere near what I've established with Chastity.

Just not having to hide anything was what I appreciated the most. I was going to tell Averly about this too.

I hope I'm not risking it all for nothing, though. The back and forth with Averly is so confusing.

I did my best to clear my mind as much as I could on the way back to the mansion.

"Boss, I don't know if it was cool or not to tell Averly where you were, but the way you are with her, I felt it was a good call to tell her."

"You did right. I'm not trying to hide anything from her. This has been hard for both of us. We both are putting a lot on the line. I just need her to know that my loyalty is with her now."

"Just give it time. You're different with her. Y'all be looking all deep in each other's eyes and whatnot," he laughed.

"Nigga, shut up and drive!"

I was grateful that Hump broke the tension somewhat.

When I got into the mansion, I only saw Juanita. She was cleaning the lower level.

"How bad is it?"

"It's bad. What happened?"

"I'll tell you later. Send a prayer up that this woman doesn't shoot me, Juanita," I shook my head as I ascended the stairs.

I placed my hand on the gold handles of the wooden doors and slid them apart.

Averly was swaying off-beat to the music she was blasting. The top of the cognac was sitting next to the opened bottle. She was tossing shots back like a seasoned alcoholic.

"Can we talk?" I asked.

"I can't hear you," she took another sip from her glass and kept dancing as if I wasn't standing there about to burst a blood vessel.

Pop!

Pop!

She clamped her mouth shut, but her jaw went slack when she turned around, "Are you crazy?"

I was clenching my jaw so tightly that my head was starting to hurt.

Averly had a way of getting under my skin in a way I've never known was possible.

It's like she was built to get on my nerves or something.

She sluggishly went back over to her bottle of cognac and filled her glass. The initial shock of me shooting out the radio wore off quicker than I thought it would.

I blew two shots into the radio system. The smoke was thick and black. You could smell the toxins burning from the fried wires.

"If you stopped jumping to conclusions, you would've heard me explain that she called me because someone broke into the house. I'm still on the deed, so naturally, it comes back to me if anything goes down. With everything going on, I wasn't sure if someone had been there looking for me. That nigga, my daddy, fired was the one shooting at us today. I couldn't have her in the crossfire. I hope you can understand that. I only went there to make other living arrangements for her."

"I didn't know."

"Your jealousy is confusing me? One minute you're hot. The next your cold. One minute you're all over me, and the next, it's just sex. Like, what's good with it?"

"It was just a lie. It meant everything. I've been falling for you, but I'm scared. This is something I use to dream about when I was in high school. Now that I have you here in the flesh, I'm freaking out. I try to keep my guards up, but you keep breaking through. I don't take it well when people leave me. It changes me. I don't want that to happen if you decide that you don't want this anymore."

"We're in this together. I keep telling you that."

"Yeah, because we have a contract. You're not here because you want to be. I never had to worry about cheating with Grecia. That wasn't something he did. With you technically, it wouldn't be cheating."

"First of all, if I didn't want to be here, you would be able to tell. Second, I would never cheat on you. I would never do that to you. Not all street niggas lack the ability to keep their Johnson in their pants, Averly. Grecia is not the only man with a moral compass. The moment you gave your body to me that solidified things for me. We became one spiritually. On our wedding day, it will be the outward demonstration that our families have merged."

"I'm sorry for spinning out. This is all new for me."

"I ain't never had to draw up a contract for a female to rock with me. You're not the only one trying to adjust. Please, just give me the benefit of the doubt."

"I can do that. You want to go upstairs, cuddle, and watch Vikings?"

"You think Juanita still got our snacks from earlier?"

"Yes, they're in the refrigerator," Juanita chimed in from the doorway.

We both jerked our heads in the direction of her voice.

"What? I heard gunshots," she said, waving her Desert Eagle in the air.

We all started laughing.

"It's nice to see everyone in this house stay ready," I said.

"And do!" Averly laughed.

"I'll make everything fresh for you both and bring it back up," Juanita offered.

"Thank you," Averly smiled.

She was back to her old self. I was relieved. That woman was off the chain when she was upset. I'm glad I'm seeing all her season right now.

I know they're going to be surprises, but I want to limit them as much as possible. People are together for years and don't know who they're really marrying at the end of the day.

I was glad peace had been restored between us.

"You ready to make up," she smirked.

"Look at you?"

"Uh-hum," she smirked devilishly as she led me to our bedroom.

CHAPTER TEN

AVERLY GRACE

I didn't get a chance to hear Lexington's response before Amos peeled the car out of the driveway. It didn't stop me from extended my middle finger and flinging a handful of profanity at him through the open window. Amos opened the car up on the main road as if he couldn't get me home fast enough.

I stormed upstairs to the living room on our wing before anyone could stop me. I pulled the double wooden doors closed behind me.

I'm glad no one was downstairs when I came in. I didn't feel like explaining what just transpired.

I felt stupid bragging about Lexington now. As soon as I turned my back, he dipped out on me to go to his ex-girlfriend's house. I wonder how long he's been doing that?

I turned on the music and listened while I tossed back a few shots of Cognac as fast as I could without throwing up.

I poured one more as I started to sway my hips from side to side to the music. I wasn't much of a dancer because I had no rhythm, but I still enjoyed it when I was pissed off.

It turned me on when Lexington shot the radio up. I was glad he was no timid man that let me run over him.

After we showered, we curled up in the bed with the snack tray Juanita prepared for us. She also made us some lamb chops, potatoes, and asparagus.

We were starving. Our day was so adventurous we hadn't realized we didn't take the time to sit down for dinner.

Since we signed the contract, we've both been glued to the hip in a dire attempt to get to know each other the best we could.

When I woke, Lexington was already awake, kneeling beside the bed praying. It was a part of his morning routine.

He prays, reads his bible, and checks his stocks. This time I decided to kneel next to him and join him in prayer. What could it hurt?

He lifted his head slightly and wrapped his arm around me. I felt an unusual peace as he prayed softly in my ear.

It was probably his prayers that have been keeping us safe.

I closed my eyes and meditated on the words he uttered to a God I never bothered to get to know.

I wasn't an atheist or anything. We just never talked about God in our house or went to church.

"Are you ready for this wedding rehearsal and dinner tonight?" Lexington asked, helping me off the floor gently by my hand.

"As ready as I can be. All the communities are coming together tonight. I know they're going to bombard us with questions. One by one, they'll try to pick us apart," I sighed.

"All will be well. I promise," he assured me.

Lexington

"How can you promise such a thing?"

"One day, you're going to realize that I don't play about you, Averly Grace."

"I don't have time to eat. I have a lot of running around to do."

"Aht. Aht. Sit down and put something on your stomach. I'm not about to have you out here famished."

He took a seat and motioned with the wave of a hand for me to join him at the table.

I did as he asked.

"So, what all do you have to do today?"

"I need to make sure Juanita is aware the event planner will be here in a couple of hours to set up. We need to get our hair, nails, toes, etc., done."

"You don't need me, do you?"

"No love. I'm sure you would only frustrate me while I rip and run like a chicken with its head cut off. What do you have to do today?" I asked him.

"I need to make sure my father is handling the situation from yesterday. He's been trying to keep me out of everything, so we have a semblance of a courtship. I refuse to have us blindsided again. Is it okay with you?"

"Yes, do what you must. I'll handle things here. If you need anything from our family, let me know. The point of this merger is to combine our power. We can't keep acting like we're afraid to use it. It's time we suffocate our enemies with the strength of our empire."

"Gone head, Mob Wife," he let out a goofy laugh I've never heard from him before.

"I'm refuse to be out here dodging bullets every other day. If we have to make an example out of someone, that's precisely what we'll do. It's time to come spill some blood."

"Say less," a quick tug put me sitting pretty on his lap.

I cradled his face with my palm before kissing him gently on his soft lips.

"One of your eyes has a bit of green in it."

"You finally noticed," he smiled.

"Only because I feel like you are staring through me. Not that I would hold anything from you, but I couldn't if I wanted to Lexington."

"You better go before we end up back in bed," he swooped me up in his arms and ravished me with kisses.

When we broke away to catch our breath, he lifted the weight of his muscular body off of me.

"Text me if you need me," I told him.

I went across the hall to my room to get ready to start my crazy day. Pushing all the events of a traditional wedding into a matter of weeks was wearing me out. On top of that, we're dodging bullets every few days. It was a mess.

In any event, the show must go on.

*   *   *

"You look stunning," Lexington came up behind me and whispered in my ear.

I swear he always smelled so good. I just wanted to eat him up on the spot.

"Thank you."

"Look at the happy couple," Reigna of the Ferrari Mafia called out to us.

She'd been prancing around about like a newly-minted deity demanding worship from somebody—anybody. It was sickening.

"Here this slut goes," I mumbled so only Lexington could hear me.

"Hello, Regina."

"Hello. Lexington Charles, I presume? Nice to finally put a name with the face. Your name rings bells in the city."

She was eyeing him like she was starving, and he was the main course.

"It's a pleasure to meet you."

After shaking her hand, Lexington pulled me in close to him. Her stare fell to his embrace and back to us.

"If I didn't know any better, I would think you were with child or something Averly Grace. Everything seems so rushed," she smirked.

"No rush. When you know, you know. Lexington and I have known each other since high school. The stars finally aligned, and we refused to waste our second chance."

"I see. Well, with his iron fist and your strategic planning, I'm sure our community couldn't be under better leadership."

"Thank you for your support," my light sarcasm was hidden by a forced smile as she walked away.

"She was nice nasty," Lexington said when she was far enough away not to hear his shade.

"That's exactly right. As soon as my back is turned, she's going to be throwing that old used cat at you."

"You know what? I'm going in the opposite direction on that note. I'll be politicking with the rest of the guests. Let's make a good impression tonight," he kissed my cheek before walking off.

I decided to work on the other side of the room. My nerves began to fire off and coil in my stomach when I saw Antonio "Smiley" Rufino walk through the door with his clan. The nerve!

I marched over to my dad as fast as my legs would carry me.

"What are they doing here?"I caught my dad refreshing his drink at the bar.

"The least I could do was offer an invitation when you decided not to go through with the engagement with him. You know, when you decided to run off with Grecia and build a fake life."

"You know they are believed to be behind mom's murder!"

"Tonio was adamant about congratulating you in person. We have enough enemies right now. I figured this would be a good gesture."

"I bet he was," I blew out my cheeks.

"Be nice. He's headed over here," my dad left me standing there.

"Crown and Coke, please," I instructed the bartender.

"Averly Grace in the flesh," Tonio flicked his tongue.

He was such a pig. My skin crawled every time he would touch me.

Tonio creeped me out in a way I've never been able to put into words. He's the type that would put you in a basement and lie to your family about it. His dark brown eyes were cold and hollow like his soul was sucked out long ago.

"Hello, Antonio," I forced a smile.

"I should've known that Lexington would be able to make you take those running shoes off. You need to be careful, though. You're sleeping with the enemy."

"What do you mean?"

"I'll tell you what you want to know, but you have to meet me for lunch tomorrow. That's my one condition. It's the least you can do for breaking my heart Averly Grace Saccone."

"How do I know this is not just you trying to get me alone?"

"Averly, I ain't pressed behind no female, ever. I would be foul to let you marry into that family or go through with this without telling you what I know. It seems like I'm the only one willing to keep it one hundred with you. They all lying to you. Just know that."

I felt queasy after Tonio walked away.

"Are you okay?" Lexington asked.

I saw him walking over when he noticed Tonio and me talking.

"Yes."

"Is there something I need to know about him? I know the type of dude he is. Did he make you uncomfortable or anything?"

"No. He proposed to me around the time I met Grecia. The merger we made with the Mamba Mafia, his family wanted to do the same years ago, but it was complicated."

"It's complicated now," he laughed.

"Yeah, but my dad didn't give me a choice this time. You seem to be aight so far, though."

I was forcing my normalcy to keep Lexington from asking me more questions.

I was relieved he accepted my response. We both went back to networking the remainder of the night.

I tried my hardest to push what Tonio told me out of my mind. At the same time, I was anxious to find out what he knew. Was it even true? Was Tonio willing to go to any length to stop the merger of Lexington's family and me?

As soon as the last guest had left the mansion, I kicked off my shoes and picked them up.

"I'm going to head upstairs and shower," I kissed Lexington on the cheek.

"Are you sure you're okay?"

"Yeah, it's just been a long night. I just want to get some rest."

"Okay, let me make sure Juanita doesn't need any help. I'll be up shortly."

"Okay," I gently released his hand.

I took a quick shower and hurried into bed. I didn't want Lexington trying to make small talk or cuddle.

Until I found out if what Tonio had to say, I wasn't trusting anyone.

When I heard Lexington's footsteps in the hallway, I closed my eyes and played sleep.

I could feel the heat from his body as he stood over me. He planted a kiss on my chest and went into the bathroom.

I exhaled when I heard the shower come on.

He tried to spoon me when he was done, but I shift like I couldn't get comfortable until he rolled to his side of the bed.

If he had an issue, his body language didn't show it.

I purposely woke up the next morning before Lexington got up to pray and start his day.

I scribbled a note and left it near his bible. Once I was in my car, I texted Tonio to see if he could meet me for breakfast instead of lunch.

I couldn't stand to wait forever and a day for someone to tell me something they had to say.

I was relieved when he texted me back that he could. I sent him an address to a location outside of the city limits.

I watched Tonio fix his clothes as he got out of his white Corvette.

We decided to meet at an old diner. Except for a few truckers, we were the only ones there.

"Heeey V," he smiled, taking a seat.

"Hey, Tonio."

"You want something to eat?"

"Tonio, cut it out. You know why I'm here. It's not because we're old friends catching up over breakfast."

"Dang, excuse me for trying to be cordial. They killed your mom."

"Tonio, I know the Rufino Mafia killed my mother. Tell me something I don't know. Why you brought me out here to waste my time?"

"You don't believe that, or you wouldn't be here. I know deep down inside something has been telling you there's more to your mother's death. Why didn't he wipe my family out if that was the case? Your father and Dasante Charles killed your mother."

My stomach hardened like a block of cement, "Why would they do that? You're lying! They hate each other!"

"You ever asked yourself why? Your mother was messing with both of them. Your grandfather made Desante set her up. He started an affair with her just to expose her to your grandfather. This was his excuse just to get rid of her. The story went when she got pregnant with you; they made her get a DNA test. Neri is your father, but they honestly weren't sure. Neither was she. At the end of the day, they couldn't trust her. She knew things that they weren't comfortable with if she walked away. They killed her and made up some story that Riamando Rufino's family killed her as payback for not allowing them into the Bloody Five."

"My mother would never!"

"Oh, but she did. I'm not trying to be a jerk or sully your mother's memory. You know I've always been fond of you despite my reputation. I'm working on redeeming the Rufino family now. I just wanted you to know that I'm doing everything in my power to do what's right. I didn't want you blindsided or stuck in a marriage that would suffocate you. I wish you the best in a house full of snakes, though," he shrugged, picking up the menu.

"How do you know all of this?"

"Because people talk Averly. They're just not talking to you because they know the ramifications that come with it. Why do you think y'all have been so open lately? The hits? They look at your father as if he can't run his own home. How could he run five of the largest Italian families in the city? There's no way my family would be able to walk this earth if they had killed Elenor Saccone. The Council would've wiped out our bloodline for the violation. You know how this works."

I sat there stuck. What have I gotten myself into? Was my father capable of killing my mother because he couldn't have her to himself? What had my head spinning was the fact that my mother allegedly had a thing with Dasante Charles.

I needed to get to the bottom of this somehow!

CHAPTER ELEVEN

LEXINGTON CHARLES

The Wedding Day

Yesterday Averly had no idea I followed her outside of the city limits. I wanted to air that diner out when I saw Tonio pull up and join her. I asked her straight up what was going on between them last night, and she lied to my face.

We decided to sleep in separate rooms last night because today was our wedding day. The vibe between us was off. There was this unspoken tension between us—short conversations filled with a lot of dead air.

Neither one of us was bold enough to speak on it. It was like whoever spoke on it first was exposing that they cared.

We weren't about to do that.

Instead of going to my father's house to get ready, I decided to go to Chastity's to help her move. I didn't care about a wedding anymore or a contract.

I'll be there when I get there.

"Aren't you supposed to be getting married today?" Chastity smacked her lips.

"Look, do you want me to help you or not?"

"Yeah," she mumbled.

The moving crew was handling the larger items. I helped her get the small things together.

"I tried to get everything together as fast as I could."

"It's okay. I'm sorry I dragged you into all of this. Your new house is paid for in full. Only your name is on the deed. I hired a security team for you until I can be sure you're not in danger."

"Thank you. I'm pissed about how things ended between us, but I'm glad you came through for me. What will your soon-to-be wife think?"

"I don't care what she thinks about now."

"Trouble in paradise?"

"Nah, it's cool. I told you this was just business."

"Last night, you told me you were falling for her. Which is it?"

"It's none of your business, Chastity."

"I'm not your enemy Lexington," she invaded my personal space pressing her breast against my chest. "One last time for the road?"

Her hands were embedded on my chest. I wrapped mine around hers and removed them from my chest. I gently pulled them up to my lips and planted soft kisses on her knuckles.

"I thank you for being everything I needed when I needed it. I'm sorry for breaking your heart. We both know I'm not a cheater. No, I don't love her the way I loved you, but I'm committed to her now."

"Loved?"

"You should be able to take it from here," I released her hands and grabbed the last box of my belongings.

I looked back once more over my shoulder.

Chastity's face hung in sorrow. A single tear escaped her eye.

I know she was wondering how a woman I barely knew could rip us apart.

"Make sure she gets off okay," I advised her security detail before leaving.

I peeled my truck out of the driveway. Once I got on the highway, I opened it up to get to my dad's house.

Traffic was moving fast despite being crowded. All in all, I made it to my father's house within the hour.

"Where have you been?" My dad yelled from the entranceway.

"I had some business to take care of."

"You will not mess this up for me! Hurry up and get dressed so we can get to the church! You have one job! Just the one!"

I bumped his shoulder as I walked by. I wasn't in the mood for anything he had going on.

I just left the woman I knew for sure was in love with me to marry one that's consorting with my enemy. Averly Grace can't be trusted. There's no telling what she has going on.

It would explain why she's always so hot and cold. I honestly believed we were in this together.

This merger must happen. I am more determined than ever to make sure my father brings the Saccone's to their knees.

When we pulled up to the Saccone mansion, something was off.

The dark Victorian villa cast invisible hands towards our Rolls Royce, luring us nice and snug against the curb out front.

The polished wooden floors gleamed in the full sun once we walked inside.

When I walked into the house, Juanita immediately pulled me to the side, "She's not here. She left this morning and never returned. What's going on between you two?"

"I asked her about Tonio last night. She only said he proposed to her around the time she met that dude she was living with-"

"Grecia."

"Yeah, whatever his name is."

"I left it alone, but when we were in bed later that night, she was distant. I tried to cuddle up behind her, but she didn't want me touching her. We ended up sleeping on opposite sides of the bed. Her vibe was off, so that's why I decided to follow her. She met up with Tonio yesterday. If I didn't leave, I would've aired that diner out. Averly can be wishy-washy and selfish at times. Why would she meet with him? What dealings do they have, Juanita?"

"I don't know. She hasn't mentioned Antonio Rufino in years."

"We slept in separate rooms. I haven't seen or heard from Averly Grace. I got dressed at my father's house."

"Can you try to reach her? She's not answering my calls."

I nodded and pulled out my phone. I called back to back but didn't get an answer.

Out of the corner of my eye, I could see Neri high tailing it over to me, "Have you heard from her?"

"Not at all. Juanita just filled me in. She did meet with that dude Tonio the other day?"

"What is she doing talking to that snake? Ever since she refused his proposal, he's been lurking in the shadows. Come with me," he spoke through clenched jaws before walking out the front door.

Neri wasn't this bothered by Antonio at the engagement party. Why was he all riled up now about Averly speaking with him? This family has so many secrets and dirt it doesn't make sense.

"What's going on?" My father asked.

"Nobody has heard from Averly Grace all day. She's not picking up."

"Do you want me to get our people on it?" He offered.

"Let me see what Neri is on. He told me to ride with him somewhere."

"Okay, you better hurry. This marriage has to happen. You know what's on the line, son."

I'm always "son" when he wants something from me. I wouldn't blame Averly if she just took off once and for all. These people are the devil in the flesh.

"I understand, dad. I won't fail you."

"You better not! This plan is idiot-proof! There's no way even you can mess it up."

I hovered inches from his face, "I'm not your enemy or incompetent. I'm the reason this empire is still standing. Don't you ever forget that. Once I marry Averly, our union will make us the most powerful two people in this organization. I suggest you not cross me."

"Lexington, we need to go," Neri's agitated voice reminded me that I have bigger problems to resolve.

I jumped in the truck with him. Our security team rode out with us.

"Where are we going?"

"To Grecia's."

My palms were starting to sting from digging my nails into them.

"Are you kidding me?" Neri exploded.

We were parked in front of a grand two-story home. It was painted a pristine white and fronted by tall shrubs that sheltered most of the columned porch.

It was a bit Huxtable's to me. It didn't look like anything a hustler would live in. Maybe it was a part of his front. You could tell it was empty.

"When did he move?" Neri yelled out to his security detail.

They all looked like deer caught in headlights.

"We didn't know you wanted a team on him, boss," one of them was bold enough to speak.

Neri punched the air.

"So now what?" I asked him.

"Now we have to put the community in our business," he huffed.

"Let's wait to see if we can figure this out," I countered. "This marriage is supposed to be the solution, not the problem."

"We have a house filled with guests," an irritated look marred his face.

"You right. Should we imply that maybe Averly's been kidnapped? At this point, it's something we need to consider anyway. We've been getting heat from both sides lately," I reminded him.

"This is true. Yes, let' ask the community to help us locate Averly Grace."

"Okay."

I can't explain it, but somehow I felt Averly Grace wasn't in any danger.

CHAPTER TWELVE

AVERLY GRACE

The Wedding Day

I was glad Lexington slept in his room last night. We both agreed it would be best since we're supposed to get married today.

I put on my all-black workout suit and bounced. The house was dark without a soul in sight. I hurried and put some stuff in my overnight bag and bolted to my car.

I didn't know who I could trust after what Tonio told me. I wasn't marrying Lexington under shady pretenses.

All that talk about us being honest with one another, and we're in this together.

Just lies. Everyone is lying in my face. I'm sick of it!

I didn't tell Lexington, but I've still been in contact with Grecia. When he followed us back home that day, I called him to make sure he was okay.

I took it like a champ when he called me everything but a child of God and hung up in my face.

I'm taking a chance popping up at his new crib, but I don't have anything to lose anymore. He texted it to me a few weeks ago.

That let me know he still had feelings for me.

His porch light was still on, so I was hoping he slept alone last night.

I went up to the door and knocked three times in the same rhythm he did when we lived together. Always a series of three.

"Who is it?" Grecia groaned from the other side.

"It's me."

"Me, who?"

"Averly Grace," I rolled my eyes.

He knew exactly who it was on the other side of the door. He was just a jerk.

"Who?"

"Grecia, stop playing with me and open the door!"

"Don't pop up at my crib making demands," he snarked, opening his door. "How you know I ain't got nothing in my bed?"

"The only thing in that bed is old sex stains," I marched past him.

"What do you want? Ain't you getting married today?"

"How did you know?"

"Your triflin' daddy sent an invitation to my old address. It got forwarded to me."

"I need your help," I whined.

"What's wrong?"

"I'm not sure yet. I just need a few days to figure things out. I got a piece of information that has turned my life upside down."

"Want to talk about it? You know I will always protect you no matter what! I don't care if I'm pissed at you!"

"I can't yet. I just want to take my mind off of it."

"I can help you with that," he studied me with piercing scrutiny.

The closer he got, the harder it became to line my thoughts up. Every time I tried to align one, it tumbled down, scattering the rest.

"Okay."

Grecia swung me up into his arms as he drowned me with his kisses. I met his tongue and gave it teasing laps with my own.

That was the first of a total of three days I stayed with Grecia. It was like having my old life back for a moment.

We danced in the kitchen while I cooked and made love all day, every day. I didn't block Lexington or my father's number. I wanted them to worry. I wanted them to feel what it was like being lied to.

"I need to go back home today, but I refuse to deal with them sober. You want to do a bottle of Bombay with me?"

"Nah, I got things to do today. You can go ahead, though. I will take you home and have one of my guys follow in your car."

"Yeah, I would like that. I don't plan on being in any condition to drive in a few hours."

I tossed back my first glass. Then another. I kept going until I felt sick to my stomach. It didn't stop me from taking more shots.

Liquid courage was my poison for today.

"Say, man, you need to slow down. That's enough."

"Oh, so you want to control me too? Why does everyone treat me like I'm too fragile to deal with real-life?"

"Look, don't put me in a category with them niggas, ma. I'm the only one who bothered to be real with you. You need to stop cappin' like you ain't know ya' daddy be lying to you all the time."

"Mind your business."

"You are my business! You see where you came to when everything hit the fan. To me! You know what it is, Averly. We bonded for life. That nigga will never have you like I had you. Period!"

"Can you take me home now?"

"Yep. Get your crap. Don't leave nothing behind. I don't need my girl to find anything."

"Your girl?"

"Yeah, you know how many chicks were lined up to take your spot?"

"You're not a cheater. I don't believe you."

"I didn't cheat on you! That don't mean I won't play a female to get what I want."

"I see ain't no woman going to have you like I had you either," I smirked.

"For now," he tossed my bag into my arms.

I was so drunk I could care less that Grecia was taking me home after I've been missing in action for the last three days.

"Are you serious right now?" My dad ran down the steps and pulled open the truck door.

Grecia had this grin on his face the entire time.

"I took good care of her?" He laughed.

My dad snatched me out of the truck and slammed the door.

"Get inside Averly Grace Saccone. This is unacceptable!"

I clumsily walked into the house.

"Averly Grace," Juanita pulled me into a tight embrace. "We've been so worried about you!"

"I'm fine. I wish everybody quit acting like I'll break around here," I slurred.

I walked into the family room straight to the wet bar.

"It looks like you don't need anything else to drink," my dad scolded me.

"I'm grown, in case you forgot! I'm sick of you and your secrets!"

"What are you talking about?"

"You love playing dumb!"

My eyes locked with Lexington's as he stood in the doorway, "I was just leaving," he scoffed.

I quickly lifted both shoulders in a careless shrug.

"Just remember that you ruined the happiness that we could've had," his words were anchored in disappointment.

As much as I tried to act like I didn't care, I did.

"I can't trust you any more than anyone else in this house! A house full of liars and snakes!"

"Come on," I gripped my arm as he dragged me out of the balcony.

"What are you talking about?"

"There's no point in talking to you. You act just like him," I tossed an evil look over my shoulder back at my dad.

"I've been transparent about everything! I've never lied to you. You keep making the wrong assumptions about me. It's getting old fast. I'm trying to be here for you, Averly. Please let me help you. I know you can tell that I love you."

I searched his eyes. All I saw was sincerity. Everything inside was telling me to let him in.

"I met with Tonio the other day."

"I know," his voice trailed off.

"What do you mean you know?"

"I followed you the same day. I saw you. I ended up leaving. I decided to help Chastity move before I got dressed for a wedding you stood me up at."

"I had so much going on. At the engagement party, Tonio said he had something that I should know before we got married. He said, your dad and my dad killed my mother. She was messing with both of them. Your dad thought I could be his daughter."

"Wait! What?"

"It gets worse. Tonio said they both killed her because neither could trust my mom. They felt if she chose one of them, she would betray the other with the dirt she knew about each family."

"That doesn't match your mother's personality. She always exemplified class and dignity. My dad told me a different story. One that involved your grandfather being behind her murder because he felt she was making your dad weak. He became careless with the organization. My dad said that your dad's world revolved around your mom. That he was different with her."

"That's more plausible than her dating two men and them killing her to silence her. Or they both could be lying."

"I promise you I will help you get to the bottom of this. I meant what I said. We're in this together—us against the world Averly. You can't disappear every time things get hard. You have to come to me. Give me the benefit of the doubt."

"I'm just not used to having anyone but Juanita to support me. After she was transferred to our summer house, I didn't have her for the longest. She just got back. I honestly feel like I'm losing myself."

"I would never allow that to happen. If this is going to work, you have to let me know what's going on with you."

"I know. I can't believe I missed my own wedding."

"All that planning and running around, and you didn't even stunt. Do you still even want to marry me?"

His puppy dog eyes made me believe him.

"I think our marriage is the only way to protect the community from our father's. They both are out of their minds."

"I'll do some digging on our side. You can depend on me, Averly. You're not alone anymore. We formed a bond years ago. This marriage proposal reignited it and strengthened it. You're in no condition to do anything today but are you down to marry a black king tomorrow or what?"

"Yeah, I am," I smiled.

*   *   *

THE NEXT DAY. I met Lexington in the hallway dressed in my mother's wedding dress. I'm not sure why I never thought to wear it before, but it was symbolic of my commitment to finding out who took her from me.

"You look breathtaking," Lexington's mouth slacked in shock.

"Thank you. It was my mother's."

"Are you ready?"

"Yes," I extended my hand.

Lexington pulled me in close and hooked my arm around his.

We decided to just go down to the courthouse. No theatrics. Just me and him making our vows before a judge and God.

Yesterday, we promised to have each other's back. Knowing that I can count on him means the world to me.

I've been taking him through the wringer, subconsciously trying to see if he will run at first sight of trouble.

Lexington has been solid through it all. He's making an effort to see what's going on with me. He looks past my actions and deals with my heart.

Being with Grecia made me realize that he was familiar but no longer my forever. Honestly, he never was. It's one of the reasons I never pressed our three-year engagement. He was right, and I never loved him the way that a woman should love her husband.

When I'm with Lexington, there's no doubt in my mind that he will do whatever to make sure I'm good. He's firm but loving. A killer, but he prays every morning to a God he trusts in. He's thoughtful, and family is everything to him, just as it is to me. I couldn't be happier with my decision.

We sat on the wooden bench with three other couples waiting for our turn.

I gently placed my hand on his bouncing right leg.

"Are you okay?"

"Yeah, I'm just trying to process that I'm about to be a husband."

"Are you scared?"

"Scared? Girl, bye," he laughed. "I pray I can be everything you need me to be, that's all. You've had so many people in your life fail you. I'll die before I become one of them. I don't care if we have to isolate ourselves unless we're doing business. I'm cool with that. You're all I need, Averly. My dad has made me feel like a failure all my life. When I'm with you, I feel like a champion. Like nothing is impossible. You don't make me feel like my best isn't enough. Just know that I've found something in you that's irreplaceable as well, Averly Grace Saccone."

"Averly Grace Saccone and Lexington Charles," the clerk called our names.

The warm exchange of each other's breath was put on pause.

"I guess my next kiss will be from my wife," he smiled.

We stood before the plump bald judge who peered over his glasses at us. We repeated after him the vows he read.

"Can I add something?" I asked the judge.

"Sure."

"Lexington, I vow to keep it real and never lie to you. I vow never to keep you in the dark because you are my light. You are my saving grace, and I will love you forever."

"That's the first time you admitted that," he licked his bottom lip.

I didn't miss the judge cutting his eyes at us. I could imagine he was thinking, *"They getting married and she ain't never told this nigga she loves him?"*

"I have something to say as well. I vow to protect you until my last breath. There is no me without you, Averly Grace. You have shown me that I'm worthy of love and to be loved properly. It hasn't been perfect, but it's been us. Authentically. I vow never to keep you in the dark or lie to you. I vow never to treat you as if you will break but make sure I never let you fall. I got you always and forever. Even after that."

"If that is all, you may kiss your bride. I now pronounce you Mr. and Mrs. Lexington Charles."

I grabbed the bottom of his chip as I slid my tongue down his throat. Desire burned a hot spot in the pit of my belly until he pulled free of me.

"Watch out now, woman," he huffed.

I blushed, watching him fix his pants when we turned around. The clerk standing near the door gave me a thumbs up.

We didn't let anyone come with us, but we agreed to dinner later tonight with the communities.

Lexington showered each other with hungry kisses as the shadows from the maze of trees covered us.

Amos ignored us. We hung a sharp right.

"This is not the way home," I alerted Amos.

"Chill out. I have a surprise for my wife," Lexington corrected me.

My mouth dropped when the winding dirt road finally opened up to a home. It was edgy and had ceiling to floor glass windows throughout. It sat in the middle of nowhere, so the exposure didn't matter.

"It's beautiful."

"We never got around to me showing it to you, so I took a leap of faith. Do you like it?"

"I love it. It's secluded, but the architecture is magnificent."

"Let me show you the inside. I didn't decorate. I left that to you."

"I'm going to have so much fun making this our home. It's going to feel so good being out of my father's house again."

Lexington just laughed, "Let me show you upstairs."

"What up there? The bedrooms?"

"Among other things."

I was immediately in tears when I got to the top of the stairs. Lexington had a picture of my mother hanging in the family room.

"I was missing my mama today too. I know she would've made a big fuss over us. I remember my first day at your home how her picture stood out on the wall. It seemed like you could still feel her presence. It was peaceful. I wanted that in our home. You know I couldn't forget my mama as well."

He never talked about his mom. I always wondered if he had a good relationship with her.

"Thank you, baby. You never talk about your mom."

She died before I had time to prepare myself. I don't like talking about her. It breaks my heart.

"I have one more thing to show you," he quickly changed the subject.

He helped me out the back entrance. Even with my shoes on, the grass felt like a plush green carpet.

I didn't see anything special about the greenhouse until we walked inside.

"Lexington. How?"

Bleeding heart flowers filled the greenhouse. Some were in full bloom others were just starting.

"I've hired a botanist to care for them."

"Why not just a florist?" I asked.

"Because these plants can't be grown over here unless the conditions are recreated down to the T."

"Oh, I didn't know. You didn't have to go through all that trouble."

"It's no trouble at all."

We didn't care that Amos was in the car waiting for us. We couldn't wait to make love as husband and wife. I admit that I missed this man. I finally made up in my mind to give myself completely over to him.

"Just a quickie, babe," I seductively whispered in his ear.

"Uh-hum," he moaned. "They can wait."

Once we had our temporary fix, we took a quick shower.

"Don't bother putting on any underwear. As soon as we're done with this dinner, it's going down."

We both had a guilty grin on our faces when we got back in the truck. All of the guests were already there when we arrived.

"They're already seated and waiting on you two," Juanita escorted us to the ballroom.

Both of our fathers had this look of satisfaction on their faces as if their plan was finalized. Little did they know that my husband and I have hijacked it.

They gave us a standing ovation as we took our seats at the table. Lexington and I sat at the head side by side.

"Let's make a toast before we dine," I said, raising my glass. "I apologize for my absence a few days ago, but I came across some startling news. There is a snake in our midst, and I fully plan on finding out who it is."

Lexington stood up next to me with his glass in hand, "And when she does, I'm taking their life." He searched the room until he locked in with our fathers, "I don't care who it is!" He barked.

CHAPTER THIRTEEN

LEXINGTON CHARLES

The Honeymoon

I surprised Averly Grace by taking her to an isolated cabin in Grapeland, Texas. It was only a few hours away, but it allowed her not to have our security team with us. We just wanted some time to unwind and be regular people for a bit.

"Do you know how to hike?" I asked Averly.

"No. I haven't done anything adventurous. I've never been out of the country either. Not because I don't want to, but my dad wouldn't allow me to."

"Well, all that is about to change. Your husband is going to open you up to a whole new world," I smiled at her.

She returned one, but her gaze returned to the outside scenery we passed on our drive.

"What's wrong, baby?"

"Just wondering what happened to my mom. I keep trying to push it out of my mind, but I can't rest until I find out what's real and what a lie."

"I promised you I would help you, and I mean that. For now, try to enjoy your honeymoon, baby. I got something for you in the bag in the back seat. Go ahead and get it."

"What are you up to?"

"Just a little something to help you unwind."

I grabbed his leather duffle bag from the seat behind us.

"What am I looking for?"

"Grabbed one of the jars."

"What is this, Lexington?" She chuckled as she held the clear liquid up to the sun.

"It's moonshine. You know my grandfather made the best in Texas. It's the foundation of our family's wealth. It's going to put you down, so don't be hitting it all hard," I warned her.

"I ain't no lightweight. Please believe me," she jerked her neck to the side.

"Alright, that's you. I'm not showing you any mercy just because you're drunk either. I'm taking full advantage of that body. It belongs to me now."

"I'm not taking any pity on you either. I'm a different person when I drink," she gulped the moonshine.

"I've seen that, but don't be no angry drunk tonight," I cut my eyes at her.

"Nah, I'm good. I talked to you about everything that was bothering me. We're good, baby."

When we pulled up to the wood cabin, it was breathtaking.

It faced a calm lake that was surrounded by a few trees. There was a picnic table and a pit near the bank.

Averly dropped her purse on the table and explored the cabin.

"This is amazing," she let out a winded sigh.

I stood behind her and kissed her neck. Our bedroom had a window the length of the room that overlooked the lake. When the sun would rise, we could watch it from the bed.

"I'm glad you like it. I was nervous that you wouldn't. I'm still trying to get familiar with what you dislike."

"Well, so far, so good," she beamed.

"Do you know how to fish?" I asked her.

"Not really," she shrugged.

"Well, I'm going to teach you. We also have access to the boat. Everything is at our disposal."

"Great. Can we go fishing in the morning?"

"That's the plan," I told her. "Are you hungry?" I pushed her hair from her face.

"I'm okay. This drink is hitting the spot," she raised it in the air.

"Dang, can I drink with you?"

"Absolutely. I plan on using that body up," she flashed a devious grin.

"Well, I picked up a few groceries just in case we get hungry later. There aren't many restaurants here, but there is a winery and a place nearby that has some arts and crafts classes."

"Interesting."

We kicked off our shoes and curled up in the bed. We watched the birds swoop down on the water, looking for prey as the sun slowly disappeared behind the trees.

Averly slowly unbuttoned my shirt, "I want to lay on your chest and listen to your heart."

"Okay, baby. Whatever you want."

What started as just my shirt coming off ended up with us completely naked ravishing one another.

Once we were done exploring one another's bodies, I wrapped her in my arms. It was important to me that she felt protected and safe at all times.

"How many children do you want?" She questioned.

"How many will you give me?"

"At least three."

"Really?"

"Yeah, I hated being the only child. It would've been nice to have a sibling to lean on or talk to. Just being alone with my dad warped my perception of the world and men."

"How so?"

"He's very manipulative, selfish, and his love has stipulations, you know. I love him because for the longest we were, all we had. When my mother-"

She stopped talking abruptly like the memory ripped open her heart again.

"I get it."

"What about you?" She asked.

"I loved being an only child for the simple fact that I was glad no else had to suffer at the hands of my father."

"Suffer?"

"I don't know any other way to say it. No matter how perfect I am, it's never good enough. Everything I did in our organization, he took the credit for it. Even with marrying you, he did it to further his vision for our family. I'm grateful that this time he got it right. I know we're still working out the kinks, but you've given me a new outlook on things. I can see us ruling both families with an iron fist. No one would be able to come against us."

"I feel the same way. I kept running from you because I thought you would leave me hanging again as you did all those years ago. You proved yourself to me over and over. I believe I can trust you."

"You can. Can I trust you?"

I wanted to ask her what went down between her and Grecia during those three days. I decided against it to keep the peace. A part of me didn't want to know. It's better to just keep it in the past where it belongs.

"You can."

I gently kissed her cheek as she drifted off to sleep.

I had something special planned for my new bride.

*   *   *

"Get up," Averly stood over me dressed in what looked like a Dora the Explorer outfit gone wrong.

"What is that you have on?" I covered my mouth to try and mask my laughter.

"Shut up," she tossed the pillow at my head. "This is the fishing outfit I brought," she twirled in a circle.

"You look adorable."

"Thank you. Now get dressed. The early bird gets the worm."

"Girl, it's not like you're going to be out there doing some major fishing."

"Want to bet?"

"Girl, I heard you up listening to those YouTube fishing videos last night."

"Mind your business, sir. I got this."

"We'll see."

I pulled on some jeans and a worn t-shirt. The new fishing boots were a bit tight but not unbearable.

I've been so busy working for my father it's been months since I've been able to get away and fish.

Averly was walking all fast like she was trying to be the first in line when the club opens.

I pulled the container of earthworms out of my fishing bag.

"What is that?"

"Oh, your YouTube videos didn't show you that?"

"They used artificial bait," she whined.

"Nah guh, we using fresh bait around here," I snickered.

I pulled out the juiciest worm I could find in the container and held it up in the air. It squirmed and wrapped itself around my finger.

"What is that green stuff oozing out of it?" The center of her nose wrinkled.

"It's something they do as a defense mechanism."

"That's gross."

"Now you flew down here like you knew what you were doing, now look at you," I shook my head.

We both hooked our lines and added our weights.

"You don't need a whole worm. Just break a piece off and put the rest of it back in the container."

"What?"

"Um, you not about to use all the worms up putting the whole thing on there, Averly."

I reached into the container and grabbed a worm, "Here."

"I'm not tearing his body apart," she stuck her tongue out of her mouth like she was about to throw up.

"All that cappin'."

"Nah, I got it," she huffed.

I watched her reach into her fanny pack and pull out her switchblade.

"What are you about to do with that?"

She didn't respond. I watched her grab the worm and lay it on the wooden deck. Carefully she sliced a piece of the body off and put the rest back in the container as I instructed.

Her face twisted in disgust as black chunks squirted from the opening.

"Now, if you don't catch anything, then we won't be eating tonight," I teased her.

"I packed myself some snacks. I bet I don't starve."

"We'll see. Just don't catch you something and see what happens."

Averly propped her fishing rod upon the wood railing and pulled out a book.

"Um, what are you doing?"

"Catching up on some reading. Why wassup?"

"Girl, if a fish hit the line, it's going to take your entire reel in the water."

"Ain't nothing gone-"

Before she could finish her sentence, whatever hit her line was taking it with it.

"Lex heeelllpp," she cried, trying to catch hold of it.

I stood behind her, and so we could try to get control of it.

We wrestled a bit before we were able to reel it in. "Girl, that's a nice-sized catfish!"

Before the sun was fully raised in the sky, we had a nice amount of fish. We didn't want to catch more than we were willing to clean.

"If you clean them, I will cook them," Averly offered.

"That's a deal."

I took the fish down to the cleaning station under the cabin. I tossed our catch of the day into the sink.

It didn't take me long to clean everything. When I made it back upstairs, Averly had cleaned up and had the cooking oil heating up in the cast iron skillet.

"What you know about that cast iron girl?" I asked her.

"I may can't fish, but I can cook."

"Okay, let me find out. I'll check you out once I'm done cleaning up. Here's the fish. I have stuff for a salad in the refrigerator as well."

"I saw it. I got this."

After about thirty minutes, the kitchen was smelling like a soul food seafood kitchen. The golden-brown fish was crispy. Averly cut up some homemade fries.

"Here, taste this," she shoved the hot fish in my mouth.

"Dang, you couldn't cool it off some first?" I huffed, tossing the fish around, trying to cool it off in my mouth.

"My bad. I just wanted to prove I could cook."

"You sure can. This fire!"

"Told you."

I noticed when the food was done, she didn't make her a plate.

"You trying to kill me or something?"

"No, I don't eat when I cook."

"Well, we're changing that," I stood to fix her a plate.

"I can't eat my own cooking. It's been that way since I learned how."

"Just try for me, okay?"

Reluctantly, she put a piece of fish in her mouth, "This is fire."

"Here, try this," I slid the Tobasco sauce over to her.

She put a couple of shakes on her fish. She lit up when she put a piece with some bread in her mouth.

Before we knew it, our plates were empty and our stomachs full.

"You better get some rest. I have a crotchet class scheduled for us in the morning."

"Crochet? Do I look like someone's granny to you?" She exclaimed.

I just shook my head, "It's time to expand what you're accustomed to. I haven't lead you wrong yet."

"There's a first time for everything," she rolled her eyes.

*   *   *

2 Months Later

"Babe, hurry up before we're late!" I scolded Averly.

Averly wanted to keep going to crochet classes which shocked me. She needed an outlet. Besides, her father never let her do anything. She was discovering her hidden talents.

In such a short period, the communities were thriving and making more money than they ever did when our fathers were in charge. They loved this merger because it made their pockets fat and could now leave a legacy for their children.

Averly and I agreed that as long as people had money and were treated fairly, we would have their loyalty. We were being strategic about building up the walls with those around us.

I ushered her into the car so that we could be on time. I despised being late.

"You like it, baby?" She turned to me.

Averly beamed with pride as she held up a hat she finished in her previous session.

"It's dope."

"I'm glad you like it because it's for you. I'm about to start on the scarf tonight," she fumbled through her bag and pulled out her yarn and needles.

The instructor played soft jazz music and burned lemongrass scented candles. It was so relaxing.

We haven't been having issues with the business or within our marriage, so this was the vibe we've become accustomed to.

Averly's notification for a text message went off, causing us both to look down at it.

The only thing I saw was "*BOOM*" flash across the screen from Tonio.

It was like everything was in slow motion. The next thing we knew, cars were pulling up.

"Get down!" Averly screamed at the top of her lungs to the other six people in the small room.

TAK!

TAK!

TAK!

TAK!

POP!

POP!

POP!

There was an orchestra of bullets being released. The rest of the students in the class cowered behind whatever they could find.

Averly and I returned fire, but we only had two tools each. We weren't prepared for a full-blown shoot-out.

"I'm out," Averly looked at me with terror in her eyes.

"So am I," I panted.

Suddenly, the gunfire ceased. You could hear a pin drop.

I peeked my head slightly above the counter to see what was going on.

Tonio's father, Rimando, walked into the bullet-ridden building.

When we noticed he was unarmed, we stood up to face him.

"If you shoot me, it will be an act of war," he warned us.

"It's already an act of war when you opened fire on us!" I spat.

"Trust me. You have no idea how far I'm willing to take this. For far too long, we've been getting the bad end of the stick. We've been blamed for blood we didn't shed. That lie has made our business starve and dry out. We're scrabbling like animals just to get what we deserve. We are tired. We will be vindicated one way or another. You two can kill your fathers and right this wrong, or I will rain down hellfire on all of you. We have nothing else to lose. You have seven days to get it done. Just so you know, we have moles inside your organization. This has been in the works for years. I've been planning my revenge since the day your mother was killed."

"Is it true?" Averly blurted out.

"Is what true?" Rimando responded.

"Did our fathers kill my mother?"

"Yes."

Without warning, Averly's vomit splattered everywhere, including on my shoes.

The people from the class were still huddled in the corner, afraid to draw attention to themselves in fear of being killed.

"Seven days," Rimando reiterated.

I wasn't for all the talking. The only thing I cared about was getting revenge. I don't care if we go through with killing our fathers or not. I'm tired of people thinking they can shoot at us and get away with it. We ain't soft and that's exactly how they're treating us!

We have been moving carelessly. Things have been so good that we thought even our enemies were at peace with us. We were wrong, and it could've easily cost our life.

They left as quickly as they came. Once the coast was clear, I ushered Averly over to a chair to sit down.

"Are you okay?" I asked her.

"Yeah, I just need to get some rest."

"Agreed. We will figure out how to kill all of them tomorrow. Let me check on these people and see how much this is going to cost to keep quiet."

"I told you this was a bad idea!" Hump was livid once he arrived. I texted him about what went down because I didn't want to hear his mouth. "Y'all both been out here moving like people not still out to get at y'all! Y'all two of the most powerful people in this city right now! I don't care how quiet things get. It ain't never that sweet!"

I ignored him while he checked on the other people who were in the shootout.

"I'm sorry about all of this. I'll pay for everything. Are you all okay?"

The horrified group was still in shock. Hump walked over and handed me a briefcase. I opened it and gave them each a bundle of money that contained ten thousand dollars.

"This is for you," I handed the sweet owner thirty-thousand dollars. "I would appreciate it if the authorities weren't involved."

"I understand completely," she bobbed her head up and down.

Her fear quickly subsided when she saw the money.

"Here is my card. Can you please contact me with an estimate for the damages? I will cover everything. Feel free to consider any upgrades you may require."

"Thank you. I will."

"Hump have the rest of the men help her get this place boarded up."

"Okay, boss."

Hump signaled for some of the crew to assist her while the rest stood guard.

Once he gave them their orders, he watched us get in our car. He personally followed us home with a few of our henchmen.

Averly's phone was blowing up. It was her father.

"Isn't it odd that he always immediately finds out we've been in a shootout?" I asked Averly.

"Very," she sighed, ignoring his call.

"We've been in our love bubble, but we can't avoid this any longer. It's time we find out the truth about what happened to your mother. Especially if it's putting targets on our back. Rimando's clan is just as big as ours. Then he was saying he has moles planted within our organizations. I'm not feeling that!"

"Me either. We need to figure out a way to flush them out. Ain't no way I'm going to be at the mercy of Rimando," she snapped.

One thing about Averly, she hated when her back was against the wall. She was going to come out swinging no matter what.

"I'll go talk to my dad tomorrow to see what I can find out."

I still didn't tell my wife about the story my dad told me. He said her grandfather hired him to kill her mother for a seat at the table.

I haven't told her because I didn't want to send her on a wild goose chase. I also didn't want to kill my father. I would if I had to, but I'd rather not. Like Averly, my father was all I had.

If I find out either of them is trying to sabotage my wife and me, I will kill them without hesitation. I cringed at the thought of my dad dying at my hands, but it is what it is.

CHAPTER FOURTEEN

AVERLY GRACE

My father sent Juanita over to check on me since I ignored his calls last night.

"You know he worries about you," she fussed as she followed me inside of the house.

I curled back up on the couch. I was still feeling nauseated. Lexington left early this morning to talk to his father as promised.

"I know Juanita, but I can't deal with daddy right now. I have a lot on my mind. We just got everything settled in the community; now we have to deal with Rimando and his clan."

"Are you sure it's just stress? When was the last time you came on?"

I laid there tossing my eyes from side to side. I've been so busy since the honeymoon I didn't pay attention. Lexington and I have been sexin' like crazy.

"It's been a while, but I've been stressed. You know I've been having a lot going on."

"Come," she waved for Lily. "Take this and get three pregnancy tests from the pharmacy."

Lily nodded as she took the money from Juanita's hand.

"Juanita, I can pay for that."

"Hush. I got you."

"I can't be pregnant. This is not the right time to bring a baby into this world. We were just in a shoot-out the other day!"

"Calm down. You survived just fine."

"Yeah, but my dad didn't have me in the middle of shootouts! Even after mom died."

"You have just too young to remember."

"What?"

"Yes, right after your mother gave birth, Dasante's clan shot up one of your father's restaurants. He and your mother were inside with you. I was shocked when he proposed that you and Lexington marry, but nothing ever ceases to amaze me with your father."

"The only thing he will compromise for is his money. He doesn't care about anything else," I assured Juanita.

"He cares about you. He just has a hard way of showing it. I know at times it may appear that his callous to your feelings. Your father will die for you. You must know at least that?"

"My father would sacrifice my life before he would lay down his. That's what I believe. Lexington has been the only one in my life outside of you I've been able to trust. I hate what it would do to him if I am pregnant."

"What do you mean?"

"When I was gone those three days, I was with Grecia. We had sex a few times."

"Unprotected?"

I was silent momentarily. I always stood on anything I did, right or wrong.

"Yeah."

"Averly," she sighed.

"I know. I was drunk and mad. I didn't care at the time. I didn't think I could get pregnant. We've had slip-ups plenty of times. I never got pregnant. Even when I was trying, I didn't get pregnant by Grecia."

"It usually happens that way."

"What am I going to do? You know I'm not a liar. I have to tell my husband that it's a possibility that the baby is not his."

"I understand. I would never tell you to do anything different. Lexington has the right to know."

I drank more of the bottled water I had sitting on the stand next to me.

"Here you go," Lily burst through the doors smiling from ear to ear.

I sorrowfully took the bag from her and went into the downstairs bathroom. I tossed it on the counter and internally cursed the day I was born. I can't be someone's mother. I'm a mess.

I opened all three tests and placed them on the shelf next to the toilet.

My full bladder did as it was supposed to once I sat down. I placed each stick in the stream of fluid one at a time.

Those Kegel exercises were paying off because I was stopping that flow like a pro.

I place each one back on the side on a piece of paper towel one by one.

I wiped, flushed, and washed my hands. I remember during our honeymoon how Lexington told me he wanted to feel special if I ever told him I was pregnant.

I couldn't fulfill his full fantasy because I'm sure that part, where it may be someone else's baby, was not in the picture.

I hated hurting him. He's been working so hard with me on expressing my emotions and talking to him about everything.

After discovering our father's secret, I promised him I wouldn't leave him in the dark that we would overcome everything together. Right or wrong.

I sluggishly walked over to the pissy sticks. They all stared back like bald-headed unwanted triplets. I was indeed pregnant.

I rolled them up in the paper towel and stuffed them in the box.

"Yep, I'm pregnant," I sighed.

"Yes!" Juanita sang.

Lily twirled in a circle, "Not to speak out of turn, Mrs. Charles, but I'm so excited for you."

"Thank you, Lily, but I'm sure I don't have to tell you that what you've heard here doesn't leave this room."

"Goes without saying, madam," she assured me.

"That will be all, Lily. Wait! Have a tray of chocolate-covered fruit from Edible Arrangements sent here. Get the largest one they have too. If I need anything else, I will let you know."

She nodded before disappearing out of the room.

"How do you feel?" Juanita pried."

"I'm not sure. Confused. Worried. Nervous."

"All valid emotions."

"Juanita, can you call that restaurant downtown to set reservations for Lexington and me?"

"Sure. Do you need anything else?"

"Hey, my love," Lexington walked into the room, startling us both.

"Hey baby," I kissed him.

"Hey Juanita," he kissed her on the cheek as well.

They got close while he stayed at my father's house. I was grateful down the road he had her to help ease his transition into the family.

He later told me how she would give him pointers to get and stay in my good graces.

I was a handful. At this point, I was just glad that he didn't give up on me. I'm not sure if he will want to stick by my side after revealing my truth, but I had to try.

One thing I promised him was that I wouldn't lie to him about anything.

"Are you okay, baby? You look flushed?" He questioned, caressing my cheeks.

"Just a bit stressed. Juanita is making reservations for dinner downtown later. I just want to unwind and let my hair down."

"Anything you want. I'll let Hump know so the security team can make sure everything is in order before we arrive. The next person who thinks they can shoot at us finds out that the old me is still alive and in the flesh. The only reason I haven't touched Tonio and his father is because of you. We still need to come up with an end game. Ain't no way we can let them slide with shooting at us."

"I know, baby but not right now. Let's just destress for now."

"Agreed."

"Ma'am. They'll be here within the hour,' Lily informed me.

"Who will be here in an hour?" Lexington asked.

"I have to go. I love you too. Averly Grace, I'll text you with the reservation time," Juanita got out of dodge quickly.

I was hoping that telling him I'm pregnant in a public place will keep him from snapping out on me.

"And you just get the security team in place and meet me upstairs in the shower," I seductively snaked my tongue down his throat. "Don't worry about what will be here in an hour. It's a surprise."

"Oh, most definitely!"

He hurried off to get things in order. My face fell with despair as soon as he was out of sight.

I sat down on the purple ottoman, trying to figure out what I could wear. I thought I had just gained a bit of weight, but it turns out I got a gut full of baby.

I pulled my sheer white dress from the rack. My boobs looked great, and the lower flare hid my pudge effortlessly.

I turned on the shower. The steam from the hot water quickly filled the bathroom. I stepped inside. I was immediately put at ease as the water covered my body like a security blanket.

I was so engulfed in the thoughts of the mess I've made of my life and soon to be my marriage that I didn't hear Lexington come in.

The heat from his body made me feel secure. It demanded my attention, and I obliged.

I wanted one more moment of serenity with my husband before all hell broke loose.

"You drained all of my energy, baby," Lexington struggled to catch his breath after our passionate love-making session.

"Well. You better find some because we have dinner reservations. Juanita set them for seven, so we need to get moving."

I heard a faint tap on our bedroom door.

"Who is it?" I asked.

"It's Lily, madam."

I pulled the door open. Lily was standing there with the Edible Arrangement I ordered earlier.

"Thank you, Lily," I took it from her and closed the door.

"Who sent you that?"

"It's for you, my love," I smiled, extending my arms to hand him the tray.

"For me?"

"Yes, I wanted to do something special for you. Roses seemed to be too girly. I thought this would be a nice compromise."

"I love it," he stuffed a few apples in his mouth along with some marshmallows.

"Okay, put that on pause, baby. Get dressed," I scolded him.

After concentrated effort, I was finally able to get my husband dressed and in the car.

We didn't go anywhere without security now. It was time to stop pretending we didn't live in a ruthless world where someone was always coming for our spot.

My husband waited for Amos to open his door once we arrived. He stepped out on the curb and reached his hand out to me.

I gently slid over so he could help me out. He smoothed out the back of my dress, making sure to cop a feel.

"Mr. and Mrs. Charles, we have been expecting you," the owner JoAnna greeted us at the door.

Her restaurant was one of the hottest spots in Houston. She was another black woman getting to her bag, and she didn't play.

JoAnna didn't care how much money you spent in her establishment; she didn't tolerate disrespect.

We followed her to the back, where our favorite spot was.

I positioned myself in the chair when Lexington pulled it out for me. I was so scared it felt like my heart was skipping beats.

"Would you like a bottle of your favorite?" JoAnna asked.

"Yes, please," Lexington smiled.

"I'll take water this evening JoAnna," I smiled.

She nodded before going off to give the waitress our order.

"I think I have a plan to resolve our issues with Rimando. We can-"

"I have something to tell you," I interrupted him.

"Okay," he shifted nervously in his seat. "Is everything okay, Averly?"

"I'm not sure. I'm pregnant, Lexington."

"What? Baby, that great!" He rounded the table and picked me up from the chair and twirled me in the air."

When he put me down, I took my seat.

"I'm going to be an amazing father. I promise. I'll get up with the baby. You can get as much rest as you need. I'm down to attend all the parenting and Lamaze classes too. I know most men want a boy, but honestly, I don't care what we have as long as it's healthy."

"It could be Grecia's," I blurted out.

Rage fell over his face as his eyes locked with mine.

"What did you just say?" He placed his elbows on the table and leaned forward.

"When I was gone for those three days before we got married. I slept with Grecia."

"You raw dogged this nigga then came home and had sex and married me? You sure a baby is the only thing you came home with?"

"It could be yours, Lexington. Watch how you speak to me!" I spat.

"Watch how I speak to you? Watch how I speak to you? The only reason you told me about what went down was that you could be pregnant by this nigga. He's a headache now. Can you imagine what our life will be like if he's the father of this child? Don't tell him until we have a DNA test and know for some. We don't need him staking claim to something that may not be his."

"I can't do that. Grecia has a right to know Lexington. I told you first because you're my husband."

"Like that means anything," he stood, pulling his wallet from the inside of his jacket pocket.

I watched him take several crisp hundred dollar bills and lay them on the table.

"I didn't think we would still be together after what I found out about my mother, let alone still get married. I was reckless, and that's my bad, but I promised you that I wouldn't lie to you."

"I can't believe you built me up just to break me down. You took what I told you about wanting to feel special when you told me I would be a father and made it something bitter. I'll get another ride. Amos and the rest of the security team will make sure you get home safe," he muttered before leaving at the table alone.

The tears itched my face as they rolled down my warm cheek. I was oblivious as to how I could make things right between my husband and me.

He was right. Grecia would be impossible if this child were his. He still had a right to know. I refused to take that from him.

I texted him that I needed to talk to him about something in person. He quickly responded that I could come over now.

He most likely thought he would get some cat, but he was in for a rude awakening.

Since I married my husband, I haven't looked back. Lexington Charles has been everything I needed and more.

I watched the bartender come towards our table with the gold bottle buried in perfectly shaped iced squares.

"You can give it to that table," I instructed the bartender.

"Are you sure?" She was confused by my request.

"I'm sure. Can you bring me the check, please?" I smiled.

"Sure."

I watched as JoAnna marched over to our table, "Is something wrong?"

"No," I lied, but my tears betrayed me.

"Oh, honey," she sat down in Lexington's seat.

"I've made a mess of things, JoAnna. The one man to finally love me properly, I've managed to shatter his heart into pieces."

"Awe, honey," she handed me a clean handkerchief. "I've known Mr. Charles for years now."

I shot her a glare.

"Not like that," she assured me. "He's always been an upstanding man. Respectful and dignified. Quite the opposite of his father. I'm sure whatever it is, you both can fix it."

"I hope your right. Thank you for the kind words. I need to go."

"Don't worry about the bill tonight. The drinks were on the house as far as I'm concerned. If you change your mind about wanting something to eat, just let me know. I'll have the chef prepare something and have it delivered."

"Thanks, girl," I covered my hand with hers before leaving the table.

Amos was standing outside of the back door waiting for me to get in.

Once I was inside, he got in the driver's seat, "Am I taking you home?"

"No, head towards the Galleria. I need to make a stop."

He locked eyes with me from the rear-view mirror. I quickly looked away.

"It's not what you think," my guilt made me confess about something that was harmless.

"Not my business, ma'am."

I gave him further direction as we got closer to Grecia's house. The other truck of security detail was still following us.

I knew they would tell my husband, but he knew I wasn't on anything if I'm taking them with me.

I also didn't want to chance Grecia putting his hands on me. I know old habits die hard.

"Don't worry about getting my door. I won't be long," I told Amos getting out of the car.

Grecia towered in his front door as I walked up to him.

"Look at you," he pulled me into him while nibbling on my neck.

"Stop it. I'm not here for that," I forced through the crack between him and the door.

I knew my security team was looking at me like I was on something shady for sure.

"You looking all good. Why you bring your security team with you? A nigga ain't going to do nothing to you," he grabbed a handful of my right butt cheek.

"Stop, Grecia. I'm serious. I just came by to tell you that I'm pregnant!"

"What? You been laid up with that nigga Lexington. You gone have to give me a DNA test."

"He's my husband, so technically, I was laid up with you."

"In any event. If that is my seed, I'm suing for full custody."

"What?"

"I'm not about to have my baby being raised by that nigga. You buggin' Averly."

"And you think I'm just going to allow you to take my child from me?"

"You ain't got no choice! You fold under pressure. Ain't no way you can keep my child safe. You ran off and married that soft nigga you call a husband. Y'all stay getting blasted at because the whole city knows y'all a joke. Ain't about to have my child involved with no suckas'! You always been weak. Just like yo' mama was. You see how that ended for her," he smirked.

Smack!

"Have you lost your mind? You must've to put your hands on me!" Grecia had a firm grip on my throat.

He snarled as his face disfigured with rage.

BOOM!

"Get yo' hands off of her," Lexington and our security team kicked through Grecia's door without warning.

Before Grecia could up his pistol, Lexington already had his secured between his eyes.

"It's long overdue that I teach you a lesson," Lexington growled. "Get this nigga in the truck," he instructed our team.

"Lexington, no, please," I begged him.

"You still taking up for this nigga after he just sat here and put his hands on you? You know what? Let him go y'all. Get to the truck now, Averly Grace!"

I did as my husband commanded. I know he was sick of me. I just couldn't seem to make things right. The more I tried, the more it seemed like they fell apart.

I don't know what exchange of words Lexington and Grecia had in his house, but I know it wasn't good.

"Did you tell him I was here?" I snapped at Amos when I was back in the truck.

"Mrs. Charles, your husband gave all of us strict instructions concerning you. I didn't personally let him know, but best believe someone on the security detail did. He's only trying to keep you safe, not spy on you," he tried to appease my anger.

"Take her home! Now!" Lexington yelled at Amos.

"Wait," I yelled at Amos. "Are you coming home?" I asked my husband.

"I said to get her home. Now!" He ignored me.

My husband ignored my question. I looked out the back window as his silhouette shrank the further we got down the road.

I don't know what he planned on doing to Grecia once I was gone. I hope he took into consideration that he could still be the father of this baby. All the more reason, I think Lexington would kill him.

I didn't have Juanita to cry to anymore. Just me and those four walls that were sure to talk back to me.

I watched as the security team went inside to make sure everything was clear before I entered. Hump motioned for me to come inside.

He arrived when my husband popped up at Grecia's. He sent Hump when he wanted to make sure I did what he told me to do.

"How mad is he," I asked Hump laying my purse on the table.

"Mrs. Charles, you know I don't get in y'all business."

"C'mon Hump."

"On the cool, his feelings hurt. He ain't gone say that, but I've known him since we were shorties. He hit the roof when he found out you were at that nigga house."

"You think he gone kill him?"

"I don't even know. I'd be surprised if you didn't. Grecia put his hands on you. He would feel like less of a man if he didn't set that straight."

"It's deeper than that. It's more to the story."

"Ain't no man gone let another nigga put his hands on his woman."

"I know."

"Well, he wants me to stay here with you until he gets here."

"When will that be?"

"I don't know, Averly."

I went upstairs while Hump made himself comfortable in the family room.

I think he had something going on with Lily, but I couldn't be sure.

Our bed felt cold without Lexington in it. I called and texted him over and over, but I didn't receive a response.

I got undressed and took another shower. All the water in the world couldn't wipe away the despair pulling me under like quicksand.

After an hour, I came to the painful conclusion that my husband needed some space.

I couldn't blame him. I prayed that the morning would bring new mercies to my marriage.

When I got out of the shower, I kneeled beside the bed as my husband had done so many times.

"Lord, I think that's what my husband calls you. I don't really know you like that, but my husband seems to think you have all the answers. Please watch over my husband and keep him safe. Don't let him wander over to his ex-house. If you can work this out for me, I would appreciate it. Amen."

CHAPTER FIFTEEN

LEXINGTON CHARLES

"Nigga, you think you gone put your hands on my wife and live to tell about it?"

WAP!

WAP!

WAP!

My sudden and forceful blows sent him sprawling on all fours. I could feel the bones in his face shatter as I brought my pistol across his face over and over. Blood caked his wounds, forming smudged streaks down his face.

I was already pissed my wife could be pregnant by this nigga. I was grateful for the justification this beat-down gave me.

"Nigga, you hard with all yo' people with ya.' You better kill me cause if I catch you on the streets, I'm going put your wife in that all black."

WAP!

Blood jetted in all directions when I hit him one final time in the face.

I continued to unleash my anger one blow after another.

"Nigga, I ain't gone kill you. I want you to live. I want you to plot so I can bring down the weight of my empire on your neck. I want all the smoke, my nigga! Don't let my calm demeanor fool you!" He heard me before he slipped into unconsciousness in his pool of blood.

I took the white handkerchief from my pocket and wiped his blood splatter from my hands.

The only reason I didn't kill this nigga was that I refused to make him a martyr. I wasn't about to have Averly Grace mourning her maybe baby daddy for the rest of our lives.

I understood her convictions; I just hated that she put us in this predicament. I hated feeling like I loved her more than she loved me.

Where were these convictions when she decided to lay on her back with this nigga?

I was pissed and knew it wasn't a good idea to go home to my wife in this headspace.

I had my driver take me to my father's hotel.

"Mr. Charles," the front desk clerk smiled. "What can we do for you?"

"Just my normal suite."

"For how long, sir?"

"Just for the night."

"Absolutely."

I watched as he programmed my key card for the penthouse suite.

"Do you need help with any luggage, sir?"

"No, thank you."

Once I was inside my room, I was alone with my thoughts and my heartbreak. I wasn't sure if I could raise a child that wasn't mine. I know I loved Averly with everything in me, but every time I would look at that child, all I would see is her betrayal.

The mini bar was my friend for the night. I consumed as much as I could until I blacked out.

Slivers of afternoon sunlight sliced through the curtains and left its lemon glow here and there. I stretched as I sat on the edge of the bed.

I was still fully dressed. I cleaned myself up as much as I could before going to my father's house. I still needed to find out what happened to Averly's mother. The story he told me is not the one on the streets.

"He's in his office," one of the servants told me once I arrived.

"Thank you."

I could hear my dad on the other side of the door, "I shouldn't have a problem getting him to kill her or her father. You know I've been waiting for years to take the Saccone's down."

When I heard him end the call, I knocked on the door.

"Come in," he yelled.

"Hey, son. How have you been?"

He was never this nice, so I know he had ulterior motives.

"I've been well."

"I need to talk to you about something. It's time for the next phase of our plan. It's time to take that girl and her daddy out for good."

"Do you think that's wise? We just got both communities onboard with the merger. Everyone is eating and progressing. Killing them could wreck all of that or, even worse, backfire. Their people could see this as a set-up."

"I don't care about none of that. If they want to go to war, then we can! I'm not waiting any longer to take what's mine!"

"What if I don't do it?"

"Then not only will I disown you, but I will kill you myself! You won't stand in the way of all my years of suffering and being treated like I'm nothing just because of my skin color. I'm smarter than any of them! When he came crawling to me to bail him out, I knew it was my time."

"If I'm going to kill my wife, then I need to know the truth about her mother. Did you kill her?"

My father was never at a loss for words, but now he sat before me stuck.

"There is a different story coming from the streets," I continued.

"Yeah, we killed her. We both had a different reason, but the result was the same."

"What?"

"Yes, she was the love of my life. I cared for your mother; however, the woman I truly loved refused to move on with me."

I managed to keep my poker face, but I wanted to knock his head loose from his head about the careless way he spoke about my deceased mother.

His facial expression even softened as the memory of Averly's mother.

It broke my heart to think my mother lived and died exposed to mediocre affection.

"When she had Averly, she started to feel differently about the life. After I found out Averly wasn't mine, I could care less how Neri dealt with his wife. We killed her together because we both had a vested interest to make sure what she knew died with her. Neri found out she was an informant. That sealed a bond between us that made this moment possible. In a twisted way, it made us closer."

"I can do it, but we'll have to wait. Averly is pregnant."

"That's even better! Lexington, I realized a long time ago that love makes you weak. If I was going to build an empire, it was best that I didn't indulge in it. I suggest you do the same. We can wait nine months. After that, we can rule together. I knew you wouldn't let me down, son."

At that moment, I realized that everything my father did was for his benefit. None of it was ever, so we can rule as a team like he just lied.

"Alright, I have to go, dad. I need to check in with Averly."

"Alright. I'll see you on the other side."

I gave him a fake smile and quickly exited his house. I needed to get to Averly.

He's so desperate to be on top that he will sacrifice anyone in his way. If Averly is pregnant with my child, I refuse to expose it to my father.

I barely survived that man. There's no way I would expose my child to him. If the baby isn't mine, I shudder to think what my father would do to that child just to have leverage.

I need to warn my wife as soon as possible. I wasn't about to tell my dad how I felt about her. He would either kill me or imprison me.

People think I'm an only child. The truth is people dare not bring up my brother's name. I'm not sure where my dad is keeping or if he's alive.

The Feds got him to flip on my dad, but my dad got wind of it, and no one has seen him since. He groomed Vincent, my cousin, for the Houston Police Department, but he still hasn't heard anything about my brother on the wire.

We know he's not the forgiving type. I assume my brother is dead. Before my mother died, she alluded to the fact that he was still alive somewhere. I never understood how she could just let my dad discard her son like trash. I guess she was too sick to fight him.

When I got to the house, Averly wasn't there. I called her cell, and she picked right up. When possible, I tried not to put the security team in our business. We've been doing that enough lately.

I was relieved when she picked up, "Hello."

"Baby, I'm so sorry. I was just upset. It's messing with me that Grecia could have a part of you for the rest of his life."

"I understand, baby. I'm at the grocery store right now getting something to cook for you as we speak."

"Girl, you can't cook."

"You a hater. I have some specialties," she chuckled.

"The sun is starting to go down. You're not alone, are you?"

"Um, yeah, but I'm okay."

"Where is your security?"

"Calm down, baby. Grecia went over to my dad's acting crazy with his people. He needed some reinforcements to handle the situation. I explained to your dad what's going on. He said he would let the security know it was okay to go over there. I didn't want to call you because I was afraid you would yell at me. I'm fine, baby. I promise."

"Stay there! I'm on my way!"

"Baby, I'm already in the car. Calm down. I just put the groceries in the car. You forget I can handle myself?"

"I'm not saying you can't, but you know we have a lot going on. Come straight home so we can talk."

"I'm so in love with you. Do you know that? I know it's taken me some time to get to this place, but baby, there's no other place I'd rather be. Don't worry. I'll be home soon."

"Okay, baby."

CHAPTER SIXTEEN

AVERLY GRACE

I had so much peace in my heart. Finally, surrendering to my feelings for Lexington took a weight off of me. I was finally able to see Grecia's true colors as well.

Beep.

Beep.

Beep.

The route to our house was not filled with traffic. Any cars on the road were normally passing through.

The truck behind me was riding my bumper and honking like crazy.

I knew better than to stop, so I sped up. I was about twenty miles from the house. I wasn't sure if I was going to make it.

The jeep next to me had tinted windows, so I couldn't see who was driving. It started to swerve over into my lane.

I dodged the car and sped up, but they were on me like flies to feces.

I could've shaken the one truck, but I noticed they weren't alone.

With one hard pull to the right, the Jeep finally succeeded at running me off the road.

The collision quickly formed a bleeding knot on my head. It was embedded in a headache that made my skull rattle.

They grabbed me from the car quicker than a booster snatching clothes in a blackout.

They wore masks, but there was a familiar smell on one of them. One I couldn't quite identify, though.

"Please don't hurt me! I'm pregnant!" I bargained as they tied the rag around my eyes.

The only response with a blow to the head that knocked me unconscious.

CHAPTER SEVENTEEN

LEXINGTON CHARLES

I paced back and forth, waiting for Averly to get home from the grocery store. While I was waiting, I called Hump.

"Say, why in the hell did you let my wife out of your sight?"

"Your daddy told us to go over there to help Neri out with that lil' problem that was having."

"Yeah, Averly said her dad was having issues with one of her exes," I agreed.

"No, it wasn't that dude. It was some other cats."

"Are you sure?"

"Positive, I would never forget dude's face."

"Hump, I gotta go. I need y'all back here ASAP. And take the route that Averly does when she comes back from the grocery store."

"Aight. We on the move now. Is everything okay?"

"Yeah, it's fine," I abruptly ended the call.

I didn't want to say anything yet. I think I can trust Hump, but I had to make sure first. Worst case scenario, they would see Averly stranded someone and help her.

I called her phone over and over, but she didn't pick up this time.

I grabbed my keys and hopped in my car. I had this feeling swirling in the pit of my gut. It wasn't good.

When I didn't pass Averly, I kept driving.

"Averly!" My car moaned when I slammed the gear into park. The opened door spit me out on my feet.

Averly's car was empty, but her headlights were still on, and her purse was gone.

I pulled my phone back out and called Neri, "I found Averly's car wrecked on the side of the road, but she's not here," I panicked.

I hated alerting him, but it would look more suspicious if I hadn't said anything.

"I'm on my way," was all he said before hanging up.

I called my dad. We agreed that we would wait until Averly had the baby, but I couldn't put anything past him.

I took all the control I could muster to remain calm on the phone with my dad.

"Hello," he said.

"We have a problem. I found Averly's car on the side of the road wrecked. She appears to be missing. This wasn't us, was it?"

I had to know before Neri got there.

"No, son. I told you the plan is to wait until she has our heir. I wouldn't order a hair on her head to be touched. I will find out who is behind this, I promise!"

This was the most compassion I've seen my father have in my entire life. I could imagine he saw his golden calf melt under the heat of this mess.

He was too close to seizing the empire to let it go down like this. I knew I could trust he would call in every favor he had to find my wife.

Neri pulled up at the same time as Hump and the rest of the security team. Those who were former cops examined the scene to see what they could find out.

"Who would do this?" Neri asked.

"One person comes to mind," I cut my eyes at him.

"I heard about what went down between you two. You think he would have to balls to come after my Averly Grace?"

"I don't know. You know him better than I do."

I punched the hood of my car. I felt so helpless. *Think Lexington. Think.*

She has that find my iPhone thing on her phone. I pulled up the locator and see that her phone is an hour away.

"Her phone is pinging an hour away," I slid across the hood of my car like I was a character on the Dukes of Hazzard.

"I'm not missing this," Neri jumped in the car with me. "Y'all follow," he yelled out the window to the security team.

"Half of y'all stay here. Gather anything you think is a clue and get her car towed to the warehouse. Have the team start going over it for fingerprints and anything else. Hump let Reno know wassup! I need him like yesterday on this!"

They nodded before I sped off in the direction of the red dot on the map.

Neri and I were silent the entire drive. The estimated time was an hour, but we made it in forty minutes.

When we got there, all we found was her phone.

"No!" I yelled, punching the air.

"We both know in kidnappings we only have so much time before they kill her," Neri panted, clutching his chest.

Honestly, his reaction was a bit surprising considering how fast he pawned his only child off to my father.

I guess in his own twisted toxic way; he loved his daughter.

"I know," I agreed. "My dad has our connections on this. Have you notified yours?"

"Not yet. I wanted to know what I was dealing with first. I'm on it now," Neri stepped away and got on this phone.

We had just established peace within the communities in the last two months. Hopefully, it was enough to make them want to put forth reasonable effort to help find Averly.

I needed to find her before my father's people. Now that the kidnapping is in play, it wouldn't be a shock if he used it as an opportunity to take over.

CHAPTER SEVENTEEN

AVERLY GRACE

I couldn't tell what type of vehicle I was in. The smell of weed weft off their clothes. They were careful not to say anything. We rode for what seemed like hours before we came to a stop.

They pulled me by my arm. I followed them in fear that they would harm my baby or me.

"Are you kidding me?" I spat when I saw Grecia and Tonio standing in front of me, looking like Dumb and Dumber.

"You lucky I don't dissect you like a frog and send you to that nigga piece by piece after what he did to me," Grecia mugged me.

The love he once had was gone, it seemed. His face was bruised and swollen. He still had gauze in some spots that needed to be changed because the blood had seeped through.

"Y'all niggas know each other? Are you freakin' kiddin' me?"

Grecia's attempt to block my punches failed. I caught him with an ugly right hook. Blood escaped from the split in his lip.

"Chill, man!" Tonio pushed him back when he tried to retaliate. Tonio stood between us.

"This ain't nothing new. That nigga been putting his hands on me," I spat.

Tonio gave Grecia a look that gave him pause.

"We're the ones trying to keep you safe from the people you think have your back. We're going to kill Neri, Lexington, and Dasante. All of them plotting on you in one way or another. I got Grecia to get close to you after you declined my proposal. That's why you never got a wedding date."

I cringed when I heard him say that. They have been discussing me like two jealous gossiping females.

"So did you tell him how you molded my body to your liking when we made love? Was that a part of the plan, Grecia? Was it all a facade?"

"It wasn't all fake, my saving Grace. It started that way, but a nigga fell for you for real. When I found out what they were hiding from you, I told Tonio to tell you. I knew that would snap you out of this fake happy ending you think you about to get. You deserve the truth. I told you I would protect you no matter what!"

"Even if it means handing me off to another man? Got it."

"This is the smartest move. You can marry me after we take them all out," Grecia attempted, reasoned doctoring on his face.

"I'd rather die first!"

"That can be arranged," Tonio barked.

"Tonio, you don't scare me. You've been a lame from day one. The only clout you have is from your family."

"A family that is just as powerful as your fake merged empire. Well, a little less, but we almost there! We ain't do it by flaunting around fake love either."

"It doesn't matter what you have planned. You won't get away with it!"

"Get her out of here," he demanded Grecia.

"You take orders from him? Here I was thinking you some type of boss in the streets when the whole time you an errand boy. Definitely should've killed you when I had the chance."

"You too needy to ever do it. You constantly look for someone to save you in a den full of lions. Good luck with that," he snatched me by my arm.

"So you gone let this man play daddy to your child while you do what? Standby and watch?"

"Don't you worry about all that. We got that worked out," Grecia forced me down to a cold dark basement. "I'm going to make sure my child had something you never did, both parents," he pushed me down on the couch.

"Go to hell!"

"You first," he said, heading back upstairs.

When I heard the door click, I knew I was locked away. My vision started to blur with tears. Everything I knew was a lie in one way or another. Everybody around me has ulterior motives and hidden agendas to put them on top.

My confidence in Lexington was waning. I wanted to believe he would stand on what he told me, but I just didn't know anymore.

I laid down and made love to Grecia whenever he wanted, and this man was lying to me the entire time. He was sent as a spy to push me into some warp planned.

They were right. My father did the same thing. I couldn't say for certain that Lexington's father didn't have the same plan in the works somehow.

Lexington struggles standing up to him at times. Grecia was right. I need to stop depending on someone to come and save me.

"I'll save us," I rubbed my flat stomach as I uttered promises I planned on keeping to my unborn child.

I refuse to leave my baby in this world without me. I don't care who I had to put six feet under. I wasn't about to fail my child before it could even take its first breath.

There was a half bathroom to my right. The draft in the unfinished basement made goosebumps form on my arms. It looked like the toilet had never seen a dash of bleach or Lysol.

My stomach started to roll as my guts rumbled," Please not now."

I didn't feel like throwing up in that nasty bathroom because it would only make me hurl more. Looking at what appeared to be old diarrhea and pee stains were making it nearly impossible to hold the contents of my stomach.

I found a cold corner to curl up in. I prayed it would help settle my stomach. I don't know why but the cold always had a way of bringing my body under subjection. I wrapped my arms around my body as I prayed for better days. Once my stomach stopped flopping, I laid on the dirty couch. I paled in comparison to my pillow top mattress at my new home I shared with Lexington, but it would have to do for now.

*   *   *

I looked down at my Rolex watch for the hundredth time. It had been days since I've been in this basement. They only took turns coming down to let me bathe and eat something.

From what I could tell, we were at a house out in the middle of nowhere. We had to be somewhere out in the country.

I didn't hear any other cars, people, or the hustle and bustle of the world moving around me. The only thing that can be heard was nature when I was at the table eating.

I was starting to lose hope that anyone was coming for me. I've been praying for God not to take me away from my child like he took my mama from me.

I cried not from the situation I was in but also the circumstances I was bringing my unborn child into.

"Why are y'all just keeping me in that basement?" I asked Grecia.

"Stop asking questions. Your lucky someone is looking out for you."

"That's what you call keeping me locked up in a basement? You are letting this nigga locked the mother of your child in the basement! I've been looking at you like some kind of Don in the streets, and the whole time you a follower!"

"Watch ya' mouth! I owe Tonio my life. You know you have to pay what you owe out here. Especially to them Italians! You know how they get down, Averly. Getting you pregnant solidified me with them. I had lost hope once you married that coward."

"We don't know for sure if you the father or not. Don't sit too high on your horse."

"Just eat and chill out. I'm working on trying to get you a T.V. down here or something."

"My daddy and Lexington are going to come for me. I hope when they find me, and they burn you and everything you love to the ground. I'm even sending them to ya' granny house just for what you did to me!"

Grecia rushed me and wrapped both hands around my throat. My eyes bulged out of my head. I could feel my neck pulsating underneath his fingers.

My eyes rolled in the back of my head before everything went back.

CHAPTER EIGHTEEN

LEXINGTON CHARLES

I was going crazy out of my mind looking for Averly Grace. The new house where Grecia was is now abandoned. I had my crew run through it, but we couldn't find a clue. His being missing in action let me know he had something to do with this.

I know he knew he could be the father of her unborn child. If he had her, I knew he wouldn't hurt her.

It just wasn't adding up. Why would he take her? I know we've had our run-ins, but he would rather rub it in my face than go into hiding with her.

That nigga was flashy. He liked to be seen. I couldn't see him living looking over his shoulders. He moved his granny so we couldn't use her as leverage. He moved her the same day they pulled the majority of the

security to help Neri out.

I was parked outside Tonio's bar. It was the middle of the day, but he was known for being there.

When I saw his car pull up, I jumped out.

"Hey, I don't want no smoke. I just need to ask him something," I explained to his security detail.

"Pat him down and let him in," Tonio said as he strolled by me into his bar.

After they checked me, they escorted me into the bar. It was a few people in there drinking and conversating. The bartender was an older cat. His hair was black and curly with matching thick eyebrows that hid dark eyes. I could tell he was a killer.

He eyed me as they led me back to Tonio's office.

"What can I do for you, Mr. Charles?" He grumbled, taking a seat behind his desk.

"I know Averly met with you. You told her what went down with her mom. Do you know if anyone else had it out for her?"

He was quiet for a minute as if he was thinking my question over. "Nah, other than your dad and hers. They the only ones who've been treating her like a pawn. Oh, and you are, of course. Everyone knows how loyal you are to ya' pops. I wouldn't be surprised if you did something to get rid of her."

"What? You think I want to be here?"

"I think you are trying to make it look like you had nothing to do with your wife's disappearance."

"You have no idea what you're talking about. She's pregnant man. I need to find her, so if you know anything, I would greatly appreciate it."

I was trying with all my might to keep the beast in me at bay. People were way too comfortable with trying me lately. I had to humble myself just in case he knew something that could help me find Averly.

I kept seeing me slicing his throat and writing Averly's name in blood across his desk.

"I don't know anything, man. If I hear anything, I will get word back to you. I had a thing for her back in the day. I came to your engagement party to show that it was all water under the bridge."

"You came to tell her that we all were plotting on her, which was not true. When she told me what you said, we made a pact to find out the full truth."

"You don't have to go into all that with me, man. I told you, if I hear anything, I will let you know."

I clenched my teeth so hard my jaw felt like it was about to lock up. "Nigga, I will slice your throat right now," I slammed Tonio's face down on his desk with a firm grip on the back of his neck. "You niggas think I'm a joke because I don't spray the city in y'all blood. I'll tell you what. If my wife doesn't turn up, and I mean real soon, I'm killing everyone I think had something to do with her disappearance. Since the only thing you Italians understand is violence, I'm about to rain down on all of these families! Someone knows something. I'm going to bathe in all of y'all's blood until I find my wife!"

"Man, chill," Tonio panted.

"I'll chill once my wife and child are in my arms. You spread the word that I'm coming. I'm bringing hell and judgment with me," I spat before walking out of his office.

I dipped out the side door with my finger on the gun's trigger I took off him just in case someone wanted some action.

My patience was wearing thin. With everything going on, I still found more peace at Neri's house than my own.

I figured Averly would reach out to one of us if she got the chance or got away.

"Hold on, baby. I'm going to find you," I spoke into the atmosphere, praying Averly's spirit would pick it up.

I pulled up in front of Neri's house and went inside. The place has been swarmed with security since Averly's been missing.

At first, the community didn't take it seriously after the last stunt she pulled the day of our wedding.

Once we made it clear this was not a drill, everyone demonstrated their support. They wanted their commitment to be recognized and appreciated down the road.

All leads were coming back empty. It was like Averly disappeared into thin air.

I was so pissed because she knew better than to go anywhere without her security detail.

"Mr. Charles, can I talk to you," Juanita whispered, pulling me into my bedroom.

"What is it, Juanita?"

She had me a bit unsettled. A nigga like me didn't get nervous.

"I have a confession to make," she sat on the bed, staring intently into my eyes. When my gaze locked with hers, she looked down at the floor.

"O...kay."

"I was here the night Averly's mom was murdered. I didn't witness it, but I have the footage from the inside of the garage that night. Mr. Saccone thinks it wasn't working, but I had already broken it after removing the tape. All the money that man had, he never upgraded the security system until right before you moved in."

"So did our father's murder her mom?"

"They didn't per se, take her out back and put a bullet in her head. Each had a hand in it. Both have blood on their hands for different reasons. Neri was in love with her. When he found out what was going on with your father, that love turned to hate. I can't say for sure if your father ever truly loved Elenor. All I know is that Neri's father had him set Elenor up. He felt Elenor was making Neri soft. It wasn't her, though."

"What do you mean it wasn't her?"

"Nothing. Just know that jealousy can be as cold as the grave. She also knew things that could put them away for life. I'll put it to you like this; she knew where all the bodies were."

I sat there in silence, "Why are you telling me this now?"

"That's not my confession. I just know you both have been poking around looking for answers. My confession is that I've been sleeping with Neri for years. I know everything, even the things I shouldn't. I've been gathering information on him."

"What? Why?"

"Because I'm with the F.B.I."

Her words fell dead and brittle like oak leaves in the fall.

"You're...you're...what?"

The darkening sky rumbled like an empty stomach. The thunderstorm came out of nowhere.

"I'm not after you...not anymore."

"Why are you telling me this?"

"So, you can find out what's best for you, your wife, and your unborn child," her silence pricked the sticky air and made it bleed.

I was stuck.

To be continued...